A Stopped Watch

by
Debra S. Kleinberger

PublishAmerica
Baltimore

First printing

ISBN: 1-4137-9251-0
PUBLISHED BY PUBLISHAMERICA, LLLP
www.publishamerica.com
Baltimore

Printed in the United States of America

Dedicated
With all my love to my sons,
Calvin & Hans

May you never be afraid to use your imagination!

Special Thanks to

My husband, George
for my late hours and babbling

Corinne, Dawn & Judy
for suffering through my rough drafts

Jeri, Gretchen & Barb
for believing in me

Chapter 1

Deep within the valley, nestled between the hills, the sun rose sputtering scattered rays of gold among the trees. The air was crisp and hinted of winter just around the corner. An old house stood proudly at the end of a long drive lined by trees exuding a sense of majesty and mystery. It was an amazing house and one could just imagine a face peering out from one of the dusty windows just below the peaks.

Calvin awoke, stretching languidly like a cat basking in the summer sun, tentatively wiggling a toe from beneath the heavy comforter to test the morning air. It was decidedly chilly; he let out a deep sigh and went about getting up. Calvin stooped slightly as he stood in order to compensate for the low rafters positioned just above his head. His room was situated under the eaves of the old wooden house, but that was the only drawback that he noted. He edged towards the center of the room and began to dress. His room was one of four on the second level, two of which were under the eaves. You had to traverse through his room to get to the second, a room that was not used for anything but storage. Often a noise or two would startle him and he would halt what he was doing to make certain no one was in there.

He donned a long sleeved tee and blue jeans sporting the names of some of his favorite rock bands. He sat on the edge of his bed to pull on a pair of heavy woolen socks and glancing at the frosty panes of the little window in his room he grimaced. It was cold out there and he hoped it would not interfere with the plans he had for the day. He pulled on his sneakers, which he always left tied, and pushed his dark, wavy air away from his face with another sigh and decided it was bound to be a very long day.

Rushing down rickety stairs which creaked and groaned as his weight crashed upon the worn boards he had the sensation of a prickle trickling up his neck. He twitched his neck in reflex and kept on going. The stairs were steep and narrow with only a small rail on one side to prevent an off-handed tumble. A narrow carpet rolled over the edges of the stairs, but did little to soften the sounds of the thundering feet down the narrow passage. At the bottom, the stairs ended abruptly and the hall took a sharp turn towards the left. Midway down the hall a hand-hewn door opened into another hall and the remainder of the house. Below the stairs, at the end of the hall, was another bedroom with tall slender windows that let the light in to warm the rosy colored wallpaper, lining the room. To the right of the stairs another bedroom took up residence, his parents' room. It was larger than the other two and had a large walk-in closet at the far end. Darkness prevailed in this room from the trees on the side of the house that filtered away the light from the slender windows.

Calvin didn't stop at the other rooms but bustled quickly through the entrance to the rest of the house. Just through the doorway to the right was the bathroom; the first place he would stop. He was lucky that one of his ancestors had the foresight to update the house with inside plumbing. The water was icy cold as he splashed it on his face, even in the summer though the water was cold for it was pumped to the house from where it bubbled up from an underground spring. He finished his morning preparations then headed resoundingly towards the kitchen. His stomach grumbled furiously and he found that he was famished after his long evening rest and couldn't wait for breakfast.

"Morning, Mom," he exclaimed as he bounded across the kitchen and planted a quick kiss on her cheek, "any coffee?" Calvin had been drinking coffee from an early age; he amazed most of his friends who couldn't stand the stuff.

"Morning, do you want sausage and eggs too?" His mom passed a piping hot mug of coffee his way and Calvin nodded his head vigorously at her offer. He sat down heavily at the table and watched her busily stack a plate with sizzling hot sausage and fluffy yellow eggs.

"Can I have some toast too?" Calvin asked hopefully.

"Of course," his mom replied as she plopped a couple of pieces of bread in the toaster. "Did you sleep well? The wind howled something fierce last night and woke us up from a sound sleep several times, was it bad upstairs?"

Calvin looked at her surprised. "I didn't hear a thing, must have had too much to drink last night." He laughed. He was always trying to goad his mother but she just gave him a crooked smile and shook her head.

"More likely it's because you stayed up way past your bedtime playing games on the TV. Perhaps we should move them out of your room?" She glanced at him with a twinkle in her eye then said. "No really, did you hear anything?"

He shook his head no and continued shoveling in the warm food from the plate his mom had given him. "Really, I didn't hear a thing."

His mom looked at him thoughtfully, admiring the young man he had become. He was tall and slender with well defined muscles. His dark black hair framed his oval face with wavy strands that seemed to have a will of their own. His eyes were golden, an odd color but they were sparkling and full of life. A slight shadow played upon his lip where the beginnings of a mustache loomed. He generally wore a serious expression, more manly she presumed, but she preferred the twinkle in his eyes with a smile on his face.

"What have you got on your agenda today?" she asked him.

He shrugged, hesitating to tell her too much. He didn't like for her to worry and he was afraid she might fly off the handle. "Just hanging around with Matt." Matt was his best friend; he was a lot like Calvin. Quiet, thoughtful and both liked music. Calvin played the guitar, but Matt preferred the harmonica. Matt was shorter then Calvin with sandy colored hair and blue eyes. He was a little heavier, but still held a slim physique. Calvin held back from telling his mom more.

"Where are you hanging out? Any place special?" she queried.

"Oh, just thought we might explore the barn, is that okay?" Calvin hoped that might appease her and his luck held with him.

"Okay, just make sure you wear something warm and watch out for rusty nails. There are all kinds of things on the floor and I wouldn't want you to step on one." His mom smiled gently and tousled the hair on top of his head with a playful swish.

Calvin shied away from her and put his hands up in front of his head as if protecting himself from an evil creature. "Mommmmm..." Calvin ducked away and headed for his room. "What if someone sees you?"

His mom laughed. "Out here? You've got to be kidding." She went back to her task at hand with a shake of her head and Calvin high tailed it to the door before she could get another word in edge wise.

Back in his room Calvin let out his breath and swore he saw it freeze in mid air. It was cold, but then it was also the end of October and it was generally cold this time of year. Calvin didn't mind if it was cold; he looked forward to his plans with Matt anyway. They were indeed going to explore the old barn, where the boards were weather worn and cracked and the wind whipped through the holes with a fury. Light filtered through the cracks in jagged streaks and the haze of layered dust on the old windows created an aura of creepiness. Even on a good sunny day the barn was spooky, almost as if a ghost or two would pop out of the dust encrusted walls and it did not help to think that the family cemetery was outside in the field next to the barn. The rooms were filled with an incredible assortment of old victrolas, antique tools, furniture and old trunks. One trunk in particular was the object of their quest. The trunk was very old looking and had these amazing markings on the side. It was locked with a huge bronze lock tarnished and weathered from years of neglect. There was no key. Their quest was to open that trunk.

Anxiously pacing his room, Calvin waited for Matt to arrive. He sat on the corner of his bed and strummed a few tunes on his guitar. Time seemed to pass rather slowly, but in actuality it was a matter of minutes. "Matt is here!" his mom bellowed from the bottom of the stairs. Calvin raced out of his room and bounded the stairs in a single leap. "Calvin!" his mother reprimanded, "are you trying to break the floor?" Calvin halted abruptly, shrugged nonchalantly then proceeded at his breakneck pace to meet Matt. "Put a coat on!" his mother called after him.

"Hey Matt," Calvin exclaimed as he donned a thick down jacket. The good thing about down was that if the weather did warm up, not that it was likely, it would not be too warm, yet it held out the bitter cold. "Ready?"

"You bet I am! I've been waiting for this day for a while now." Matt beamed with excitement.

"Let's go!" Calvin rallied.

The two raced in silence towards the old dilapidated building. They slid the door back on the pulleys that supported it and rushed inside sliding the door back into place to keep out the bulk of the wind, even though it meant blocking some of the light. They waited for their eyes to adjust to the dim interior. The wind howled outside, whistling furiously as it found its way through the cracks in the side of the barn. "Wow!" Matt exclaimed, "This is really cool!"

Matt had always looked at the barn from a distance. This was the first time he had actually gone inside. "Look at all this neat stuff!" he exclaimed mesmerized. His mouth did not close from where it had dropped with his first expression of awe. "Check this out," he claimed as he wandered over to an old tool, "wonder what this was used for? This place is incredible."

"Yeah, it's the greatest, come on I want to show you the trunk. The thing is like a total mystery and I've just got to see what's inside. It might take the whole day though the lock is huge and really beat up." Calvin could not contain his excitement. He led Matt through the twisted maze of stuff while Matt glanced furtively around at the inside of the run down old building.

"We could explore in here for days," Matt stated, his voice laced with excitement at the prospect. "How come we didn't come in here before?"

"I have been in here and you've always had other things to do when the weather was warm," Calvin replied as they crawled over an assortment of stuff and ducked under others, finally reaching their destination.

The trunk was situated in a back corner of an inside wall. There was junk strewn about in a haphazard fashion and they had to move quite a few things to really get at it. They tried to move the trunk out a little, but even with both of their weight thrown against it the trunk would not budge. So—resignedly—they set about moving the stuff that was in the way. Calvin shivered, not from the cold, but from that odd prickle down his neck, the same one that he had felt earlier. He couldn't seem to shake the sensation and it was beginning to annoy him.

"Calvin, check this out." Matt held a peculiar item in his hand. It was on old piece of wood twisted and gnarled with a dusty sphere at one end. It was rather long and reached up to his shoulders when he stood it on the floor.

"Hot!" Calvin replied which was the modern word for *really cool*. They looked it over carefully and Calvin marveled at the sphere on the end. With a crooked look on his face he decided it would take more than what was available to clean the years of crud off the surface of the sphere and set it down. "What else is around this thing?" They looked together at the odd pieces surrounding the trunk but didn't find anything that looked nearly as interesting besides that one piece.

Calvin's thoughts strayed from the strange object they had found and pondered the lock on the trunk. It was really large and was tarnished so that you could not make out what type it was. There was dust and dirt covering the surface. He swiped at the dirt and coughed violently at the eruption that ensued. Recovering his breath he reached out and tried to twist the lock from its hold but he knew before he tried it that it would be useless.

"This thing is solid as a rock. Matt, see if there is a pry bar somewhere, I think there may be one on the other side by the door. I seem to remember there was something over there." Matt climbed across the piles of junk to work his way towards the door.

"How 'bout this one?" Matt called, holding up a rusted strip of metal that could have been a real pry bar at one time but now resembled a broken piece of junk. The tip was broken and the rod was slightly bent but it looked as good as anything else.

"Yeah, let me try it," Calvin replied and Matt clamored back over the piles to bring the bar closer to him.

Once again the prickling sensation ran down his neck and Calvin twitched in response. He and Matt worked on the lock, but it just would not budge. Inserting the pry bar behind it they both pushed down on the bar, trying hard to make the lock snap. They pulled up on the bar, they wedged the bar in the crack around the trunk and tried the same, down then up but each attempt netted the same result, nothing. In a desperate attempt they inserted a nail and tried to pick the lock but like everything else they tried this too failed.

They turned their attention to the hinges, which were smaller and not quite as ominous looking. These too were old and covered in filth. The surface was tarnished and it was hard to distinguish where the two pieces of the hinge were fastened together. The two boys took turns slamming the bar into the hinges, but neither the hinge nor the wood would yield to the abusive assault. The screws holding the hinges in place were rusted and the heads worn so that a screwdriver could not grab enough of the screw heads to turn them out. "What's this thing made of?" Calvin grumbled. Throwing down the pry bar Calvin queried, "What else is there to use?" The two began looking through the vast assortment of archaic tools and tried several to no avail.

"I'm going back to look in the other part of the barn," Matt chimed and wended his way back in the direction from which they had come. Calvin could tell Matt's progress from the noises he made climbing over and ducking under the various assundries that were strewn about the barn and the occasional curse as he stumbled into something. He even winced a few times almost feeling the pain as Matt let out a yelp from one of his mishaps. While he waited for Matt to return Calvin turned back toward the trunk and the task of opening it.

Calvin's hand fell to the wooden piece that Matt had found earlier and he picked it back up to take a closer look. The wood was twisted and gnarled, but the surface was smooth as if sanded or worn over the years. Calvin looked about and found a dusty rag, snapping it out to remove the bulk of the crud he decided quickly that he should not have done that. The dust cloud that erupted caused him to sneeze and cough violently for several minutes. When the air finally cleared, he wadded up the rag and casually rubbed the dust from the surface of the crystal, as he did a shard of light glanced through the window, striking the sphere and cast a beam of light directly on the lock. The lock released with a pop as if it was brand new and Calvin called to Matt excitedly that it had opened. Without waiting for Matt to return, Calvin heaved up on the heavy lid. The last thing Calvin remembered was the shocked expression on Matt's face, as he ran to the trunk, before he disappeared.

Chapter 2

The sensation was one of fading, as if one moment everything was bright and clear and the next it was a hazy fog, then as quickly as it had started it ended. Calvin tried to adjust his eyes to the flickering light in the dark corridor he suddenly found himself standing in. The corridor was long and narrow with only the dancing light of scattered candles to light it.

The candles hung on earthen walls in brilliantly sculpted sconces resembling gargoyles. The hands of the gargoyles held the slender stalks of wax before their stony eyes as if mesmerized by the light the flames emitted. The walls were damp and cold, not unlike the root cellar of Calvin's old house. The floor was lined with smooth blocks of what Calvin took to be granite, and sloped downwards slightly as if it reached towards the old family cemetery. The thought made him shiver.

The passageway was warmer than the barn had been but not by much. At least the wind was not blowing to snake its way through the intricate patterns of fabric encircling him to chill the flesh beneath. He was glad that he had worn the down coat this morning, but his feet were another story. The cold damp had worked its way through his sneakers and woolen socks, leaving him with the sensation of standing on ice. Calvin reached up towards a candle, running his finger through the tiny flame and wished the flame could emit more heat. The candles glow cast an eerie array of light about the corridor and Calvin felt as though eyes were watching him.

He looked up, expecting to see the great hole that he had to have fallen through but the ceiling appeared just as solid as the rest of his surroundings. The markings that had encompassed the trunk could be seen etched periodically upon the walls and Calvin wished he knew what they meant. Visually acknowledging his surroundings, Calvin noted that a way of escape did not present itself in the proximity of where he stood, hesitantly he started walking down the corridor, wary of what lay ahead and of leaving the place he had arrived at. The twisted piece of wood forming the staff was still clutched in his hand, his knuckles turning white from the firmness of his grasp.

Loosening his hold, just enough to ease the soreness creeping into his hands, Calvin cautiously made his way down the corridor. His eyes widened after a time as the passageway opened into an octagonal room. Plaques of bronze encrusted the walls with the encryption of the same odd characters, ancient runes, a form of writing from the trunk and the wall. There was an elegantly carved kneeler with rich velvet fabric in a warm golden hue placed in the center of the room. The wood of the kneeler was dark and reminded Calvin of mahogany, the rich gleam shining like polished glass. In front of the kneeler stood what appeared to be a type of shrine with shimmering candles ensconced in crystalline glass standing on tiers in abundance. Although the candles blazed brightly there was little smoke from their flames and the air remained crisp and cool. The walls were still earthen, except where the placards hung, the rich clay damp from moisture. Small pools of water dolloped the surface of the floor like dew on the petals of a flower. From the distance he had traveled Calvin guessed he was in the old cemetery ground and this thought, the day before Halloween, gave him a decided chill; he could feel the goose-bumps rising on his flesh.

The room opened out into another passage, narrow like the one before it. Calvin once again started moving slowly down the passage. After a brief downward trek the way became flat and meandered in twists and curves not unlike the staff that he carried. Shortly the path sloped upwards and without warning stairs drew upwards in front of him. The stairs were thin and, where the passage had been smooth, the stairs bore a roughness that he supposed helped to prevent falling. The surface was worn with oval indents from what he presumed were the footsteps of many people passing up and down for what must have been many years. His hope was that this was the way out, after all he was moving up, but unlike this morning when his luck had held with his mom, there was no door leading to the outside world.

Calvin thought about his mom and a lump grew in his throat. He wished that she knew where he was and thought of all the times that she had to know of his every movement and how annoyed he had been. He wondered if she even knew that he was gone. Matt certainly would have gone for help, but what help they could have provided Calvin could not imagine. Calvin glanced at his watch. A brief look of horror crossed his face, and then amazement for the watch had stopped. It was a new watch and all the rage among his friends with a wide black band and studs encircling his narrow wrist. He was sure that it could not have just stopped, it was new, but he was also certain he had not damaged it when he faded into the passage. Now he would have no idea how much time had elapsed or if hours turned into days. Calvin's stomach grumbled noisily and he guessed that lunchtime had passed him by, which, for a growing young man who consumed immeasurable amounts of food, was something that needed to be remedied. He massaged his stomach gently with one hand the gnawing sensation churning uncontrollably with every grumble; food was now the one thought that kept him pressing on.

As the stairs wended their way up they twisted and turned almost like a spiral staircase except that they moved in one direction then the other, probably more like the curving swath of a snake slithering up a path. Periodically Calvin stopped to massage the soreness from the calves of his legs, for the stairs seemed to rise toward the heavens and even in peak physical form the stairs were a challenge to climb. After what seemed like hours the stairs abruptly stopped.

Calvin's mouth dropped in amazement; his eyes roamed the fortress of the room he now stood in. A vast room that bore elaborate columns of marble spread out before him like a great ocean compared to the tiny, narrow corridor. The gargoyle sconces were closer together here and the room did not flicker and dance in shadow. There were ornate seats scattered about the room all carved out of the rich mahogany wood and covered in shades of rich burgundy velvet. In the center was a dais intricately woven from twisting vines and entwined with satin and lace. Huge candles sat on beautiful golden pillars around the dais, radiating shining elegance everywhere.

Calvin waltzed over toward the furnishings, determined to examine every inch of this place. If the trunk was the entrance into this world perhaps another piece of furniture was the way out? Anything was worth a try and from where he stood he had nothing but time to spare. There were octagon shaped tables with marble tops and intricate carved legs that swooped in graceful curves from the inlaid top. Sofas with a rich brocade fabric glistened with silken threads twinkling within the detailed designs. He stopped in front of an ornately carved chair. The wood was dark and rich looking with intricate patterns exquisitely carved on the arms, legs and back. The velvet covering the back and seat was a deep burgundy color with the hint of a pattern in a silken thread. Calvin was amazed at the fine craftsmanship rendered in the chair and ran his hand along the surface, gently admiring the carvings so skillfully created.

What amazed Calvin, probably the most, was the small table of food that simply appeared out of thin air. The food materialized almost directly in front of him as he was examining the elegant chair. He looked about rapidly and rubbed his eyes, but the food remained. Famished as he was he sat in the chair he had been caressing, gently laying the staff against the side of the chair and began to eat, his ravenous appetite replaced his shock of the food just appearing and he did not give the sudden appearance a second thought.

Rich foods adorned heavy platters of fine china, meats with rich gravy, vegetables of various sorts, fresh fruits and to top it all off the finest of deserts. There were rich cheesecakes topped with fresh fruit, velvety cakes with whipped toppings, parfaits and an assortment of deep rich chocolates. A goblet and pitcher of icy cold water gave him refreshing courage and renewed hope.

Calvin pushed back from the table with a contented sigh and the table and dishes faded away in front of him. Satisfied, he gave a little start at the sight but with his belly full he did not give it much more than a fleeting thought. He picked up the staff from the side of the chair and walked towards the dais. The candles on each side created a shimmering elegance upon the dais where it rose above the surface of the floor. Tall columns rose upwards connected with twisting vines that caught them together with a cascade of sheer curtains that swirled down about the sides. Satin and lace caught the curtains together with delicate tendrils as it wound its way around the delicate fabric in gently curving arcs. As Calvin's eyes roamed over the workmanship of the dais he heard a soft noise to his right. He glanced quickly in that direction—a shrouded form was standing there.

Chapter 3

The person wore a rich velveteen cape of deep jade green. An intricate pattern of leaves was woven into the fabric in golden threads and soft leather boots poked out from beneath the hem. The figure was tall and slender from the way the cape draped about him, but the hooded cowl prevented Calvin from viewing the face and his nerves tensed in response.

"Are you the one who provided the food?" Calvin asked with a shaky voice. The hooded figure gave a nod of affirmation. "Thank you, thank you very much," Calvin murmured. Again the hooded figure gave a nod, and then silently motioned for Calvin to follow. After a moment to consider his options Calvin followed the cloaked figure from the room into a larger hallway well lit and warmed. The walls here were smooth and no longer bore witness to the earthen structure from which it was made. The floors still resembled polished granite with rose and silver hues. There were large doorways in this hallway, ornately carved with intricate motifs and designs. The doors slipped out of view as they proceeded down the hallway and around a bend, further and further until at last they stopped in front of a smaller door, also carved and elaborate. Calvin's chaperone turned the latch and pushed the door open and beckoned Calvin to step inside.

The door opened to a suite of rooms. A spacious sitting room greeted him with a warm burning fire in a marble fireplace, overstuffed chairs on each side and a sofa opposite buried in pillows of various shapes and sizes. On the mantle were two crystal candle holders each one held a delicate taper and a painting of a hidden spring surrounded in the mist of the morning light, nestled in a glen among the gentle woods, hung in between. The room was decorated in assorted shades of muted greens as if the forest had been brought indoors and a thick woolen carpet spread out across the stone floor. Fragrant bouquets of flowers blossomed from crystal vases set on delicate tables about the room sending a fresh aroma into the air. Calvin looked around towards his chaperone only to discover that he or she had disappeared.

To the right of the room stood a smaller door of rich wood, but this one was not carved. Calvin stepped over to it and turned the latch entering into a magical bath. The tub was sunken into the floor and the water cascaded like a waterfall into it. The stone walls were cut into steps surrounding the pool of water and each step contained bottles of lotions and soaps as well as a candle. Heavy woven towels hung from polished twisted vines very much like the staff that he carried. The other bath fixtures seemed to be built directly into the stone with carved wooden handles embellishing the surface. The room was warmed by a fireplace set in the stone wall with an elaborate bronze screen etched with vines in front of it. Calvin went back out the door and noticed another beside it. Tentatively he pushed it open.

A bedroom stood before him with a massive bed in the center. Huge columns rose from the corners of the bed with twisted vines that connected them from above. A sheer gauzy curtain hung about the bed and was pulled back on one side to show a multitude of soft pillows piled upon it. Warmth spread from a natural stone fireplace that took up the expanse of a whole wall, a wood box cut in the side held pieces of seasoned hardwood. The hearth was adorned with a heavy woolen rug and an armoire stood in the corner. Calvin walked to the armoire and pulled open the doors. Inside he found tunics with soft leather pants and full-length capes like that of his chaperone. One cape was deep red velvet with black silken threads woven in patterns throughout it and Calvin caressed the soft material, letting it flow through his fingers, the gentleness eased his spirit.

Calvin realized he was exhausted. Again he looked at his watch but still it had not moved. Not knowing what time it was, he went to the bath to clean away the grime from the day, then slipped into the soft downy bed and drifted almost instantly to sleep, a sleep full of hazy pictures, wooded cottages and gauzy figures. Sleep full of intrigue.

A Stopped Watch

Misty haze enveloped the hidden spring in the wooded glen. A quiet peace settled upon the mossy ground, the small waterfall cascading almost silently in the reflected pool of water. A whimsical cottage with a thatch roof and vines of flowers cascading about it was settled off to one side. A gauzy figure emerged from the cottage and stooped to pick something up. A flowing cape swirled among the tiny flowers carpeting the ground. Music soft and whispery wafted on the morning air in an eerie gentle song only to be shattered by an unearthly scream and a large black shadow of a winged beast soaring over the little glen.

Calvin awoke with a start, his heart beat fast and his body was cold and perspiring. Music sounded in his ears much like that of his dream. He rose and reached for his clothes only to find a tunic, leather pants, and cape from the armoire had replaced them. He wrinkled his nose, disdain washing across his face at the attire. Once on however, Calvin decided they were not all that bad, in fact, they kind of made him feel like a prince or knight. He laughed out loud at the thought. He found warm leather boots next to the bed with heavy socks to go in them and donned them quickly. The fire still blazed brightly in the fireplace and Calvin was surprised that it had not burned itself out, but then someone had been in his room as he slept, the clothes told him that much. That thought gave him an uneasy feeling.

He grabbed the cape and walked into the outer room, stopping briefly at the bath. The music could still be heard soft and mysterious. He tried the door to the hall and found it open. Pausing he turned his head to find the direction of the music then he started down the hall quickly in the hopes of finding the source of the music before it stopped. Whether luck was on his side or it was meant to be Calvin waltzed into a circular room with tall thin windows, the first he had seen since his arrival, an ornate dome ceiling was suspended by tall columns that were positioned on each side of the windows. The windows looked out across beautiful fields lit by the early morning sun whispering the arrival of the new day through a misty fog. Near one of the windows was a window seat adorned with cushions and pillows. Sitting on the seat was a beautiful girl playing a flute. Her royal blue cape draped around her shoulders with her satin gown peaking out from beneath. Her hair was golden, her face pale and she possessed the bluest eyes Calvin had ever seen. She looked up with a start then smiled gently in his direction.

"Please don't stop!" Calvin exclaimed. It had been the most hauntingly beautiful music he had ever heard.

"It is time that I must," she replied. Then in the moment that his eyes blinked, she was gone. Calvin looked around wildly and another figure materialized as if out of thin air, a cape once again draped over his head so that Calvin could not make out the face beneath, and beckoned him forward. His world had ceased to exist, what he faced now was another world, one that Calvin did not know if he wanted to be in. With no other alternative Calvin followed his chaperone carefully noting the way that they went.

This time they stopped outside the largest door Calvin had ever seen. The gold upon its surface sparkled in the light of the gargoyle's candles that lined the hallway, hinting of the royalty that must lie within the inner sanctum. The chaperone bowed deeply while opening the door and Calvin stepped through into a world he would never have dreamed.

It was as if the whole of the outdoors had come together in this room and yet among the very heart of nature were elaborate seats, columns that must have raised twenty feet and a throne upon which sat a queen. Large massive trees created a canopy with flowering vines entwined around their branches. A waterfall gently fell into a reflecting pool where water lilies opened in a beautiful array. Moss covered the floor in a rich thick carpet and light filtered through splashing rays of sun about like a crystal chandelier. The queen had long brown hair in curly tresses that hung loosely about her shoulders and cascaded down her back. Her striking green eyes seemed to pierce into Calvin's very soul and he felt as though he did not need to speak for he was certain she could read his mind. She wore a golden chiffon gown that flowed smoothly about her body with a simple gold tiara upon her head. Her smile was gracious and genuine easing his spirits with welcoming gentleness. A radiant glow surrounded her and Calvin bowed; he could not help it. The majesty of the moment swept him away with awe and he was left trembling.

"Rise, Sir Calvin!" she exclaimed. He started in surprise that she knew his name. "I am Eartheria, and you have entered the land of no time." Calvin glanced at his watch and she laughed softly. "Time does not exist here or perhaps it simply stands still." Again she laughed. "You shall witness things that your world only dreams about, some of it very, very, good and some of it evil. The most you can expect is the unexpected but know this, in due course at the end of your quest, should you survive, you will be returned to your own time. It is the only way back, there is none other." The prickling returned to Calvin's neck and he twitched his muscles, a chill coursed the length of his body. "Until that time you will remain here, timeless, wrapped within the hospitality of my people. We will protect you the best we can but your fate does not lie with us, it lies with you. Go now in peace."

Calvin knew that the interview was over and again he bowed. He had millions of questions he would like answered, but he was certain that this was not the time. He turned to leave only to be startled by other people within the room, murmuring softly amongst themselves bowing gently as his eyes roamed over the entirety of the room, then he walked softly to the door. The corridors were now filled with a multitude of people all of them dressed as he and all of them murmuring and staring as he walked among them. Somehow he managed to find his way back to his suite although to him it seemed as though it simply appeared.

Chapter 4

A table laden with food stood in the center of his suite complete with all the breakfast foods one could wish for. He realized then that he had forgotten to eat earlier, caught up with the music that still hauntingly hung in the air. He sat in an overstuffed chair in front of the fireplace and pulled the table closer to him. Helping himself to a plate of French toast, dripping with melted butter and warm maple syrup, along with sausages and scrambled eggs he dove in with unconcealed hunger. He stopped periodically to grab a piece of fresh fruit, luscious strawberries, seedless green grapes and his favorite red raspberries. To watch him you would have thought that he had not eaten in months, and yet it was only last night that he had dined almost as sumptuously for dinner. Calvin poured himself a large steaming mug of coffee, added cream, then sat back slurping it loudly and stared at the fire.

Calvin picked up the staff he had carried the day before and mused over the smoothness of the wood. It seemed cleaner than the day before and almost looked as though it had been polished. The entwined vines curved about in a manner that fit perfectly within his hands. The crystal sphere glittered with the bouncing flames of the fireplace. Calvin sighed, a deep, relaxing sigh and sank deeply into the overstuffed chair. Warm and content he stared at the picture above the mantel. The glen, he realized, was set in the mist of the morning. The light was similar to that in the queen's chambers this morning however, it was not the same location. Engrossed in the details of the painting and lulled by the fire Calvin became immersed in the scene. While his mind was focused on the painting Calvin failed to see the scene around him change, from the bedroom suite he was comfortable in to that of the actual glen. When he shook the stupor from his eyes he found himself actually lounging within the glen of the painting. His body flung across a little knoll of soft moss. Off to one side stood a familiar tiny stone cottage with a thatch roof and vines of flowers draped about it. The sound of the waterfall lilted into the air with a musical melody skipping lightly on the currents of air. Calvin's heart skipped a beat as he looked nervously about the glen wondering how he had gotten there, for there were no doorways in—or out.

The staff clutched tightly in his hand he roused from his relaxed position and took a tentative step towards the cottage then he began to run. He didn't know why, but the cabin seemed like a haven of safety in this world of unknowns and he wanted to reach it as quickly as he could. Once outside the door however, he had a different thought and he stood for several minutes, deciding what he should do before he reached out a tentative hand and knocked. The door was pulled back by an elderly man, gnarled and weathered with the ages, with white hair and beard. He was short in stature and slight in girth, his earth tone tunic and breeches were clean yet worn. His mannerism was gentle and welcoming, a knowing smile upon his face, he beckoned Calvin to come inside then closed the door.

The cabin was small, three or four rooms at best, with an odd assortment of baskets, jars, tools and herbs that hung from the ceiling. The furniture was made of crooked vines with simple wooden seats and the table was supported by four spindly vines for legs at the corners. The neat, clean little room smelled of the forest from the herbs overhead and a table in the corner held remnants of plants newly collected for drying. Light filtered in from two small round windows casting a shadow on the fireplace directly ahead. The fireplace, hearth and mantel were all made of stone, the circular mounds stacked in a perfect puzzle. A warm fire blazed within the hearth casting off the chill of the outside air.

"Sit, can I make you some tea?" the old man asked. "The kettles on the fire and you look like you could use something to steady your nerves. I'd be giving you something stronger but you look nigh old enough for that." He went to the cupboard and drew out two simple earthenware mugs and set about making tea for the two of them. Calvin watched him as he moved about the room noting his gentle mannerism. When the tea was brewed to the old man's satisfaction he handed a steamy mug to Calvin. "Drink up my boy, you'll be better off for it," he urged gently.

"Who are you?" Calvin timidly asked the old man.

"I am Logan of the Glen, keeper of the dreams and healer."

"Where am I?" Calvin once again asked.

"Why the Glen dear boy, the Glen of the Mist but, it is not where you are that troubles you so, it is why? Is it not?" the old man gestured about the cabin. "The Glen may be peaceful right now but it is in grave peril from the ghosts, the ghouls and the goblins or from the dragon's breath that bears upon it." The old man stopped to take a sip of tea. "Drink, the warmth will ease your spirits then we can talk about the things I see."

Calvin sipped on the piping hot tea letting the aromatic brew soothe the tension of his troubled mind. With every gulp he inhaled deeply of the aroma letting tendrils of the fragrant concoction weave threads of calm about his spirit, slowly the threads inhabited his sore tense muscles and massaged the stiffness away. "What's in this stuff?" Calvin asked. "It's good, really good but not like anything I have ever tasted."

"The ingredients are an ancient secret and ones that you would not be familiar with. There is much in nature that can ease your spirit, but you need to be able to know where to look." Logan perused Calvin thoughtfully and paused, "perhaps further into your quest the recipe could be told but there is much to learn before I could show you." The old man became serious, his look one of consternation. "My story is lengthy and concerns many things of which you should know, things I will tell you, when and if you are ready."

"I am ready," Calvin fumbled, not sure if he was ready or not. "I need to go home, my mom—well, she'll worry."

"Your world is as you left it—is it not? Look at your timepiece has it not stopped?" Logan watched in silence as Calvin once again looked at his watch, the hands still were not moving. "In your world," Logan continued, "it is the same. Time has not progressed since your arrival and cannot begin again until a successful end to your quest. If you should fail your time will be forever frozen at the moment where you left it, with no end to its beginning."

"And for me?" Calvin choked, trying not to think of the consequences.

"For you it would end." The statement was final.

Calvin looked intently into his mug watching the brew swirling from his last gulp, "So—what is my quest?"

"The quest is not clearly written, its outcome hinges on the choices you make. The quest began with your entrance through the portal into our world, the portal which had been closed for many years. By opening the portal you accepted the quest, when the portal is closed the quest will be finished. The ending is yours to write." Logan stared deeply into Calvin's eyes, piercing into his mind to read what thoughts were written there.

"What must I do? Where do I begin?" Calvin's thoughts were in turmoil, overwhelming questions assaulted his mind.

"Your way will come to you. Clear your mind of your troubled thoughts and follow your heart. The passion that is there will guide you." With that the old man rose from his chair, "rest, you have traveled far." Then he left the room.

The quiet of the cabin enveloped him. He drank deeply of the dark, sweet tea that remained in the earthen mug and secretly wished that there were more. What little was left did not ease the newly formed torrent that swirled in his mind. Tormented thoughts whirled in his head like a hurricane building in the southern seas. What started out as a simple matter of opening a trunk had become something more of a nightmare and Calvin's cold sweat proved it. How could he make the right choices when he knew so little of this world, this time, this place?

Picking up the staff, his only sense of security in this realm of the unknown, he moved over to the fire dancing on the hearth and knelt before it, watching the flickering flames dance across the blackened wood, charring the once majestic pieces into smoldering embers. Calvin slouched deeper in front of the flames, his elbow resting wearily on the rug with his head cupped in his hand the staff drooped across his arm lightly clutched in his one hand, his legs were bent and his body lay on his side his shoulders hunched gazing intently into the melding colors of orange, yellow and white. Where the white flames emerged, the blazing wood split into shattered fragments then broke off allowing more flames to erupt from the center beginning the process anew. The warmth of the fire, combined with the intensity of his gaze, lulled him; his eyelids grew heavy and he began to sleep.

Chapter 5

A piercing scream shattered the silence jolting Calvin from his sleep. He was no longer in the cottage of the Glen, but rather in the suites he had occupied before. With his heart racing he bolted for the door. Outside in the hall stood a girl not much older than himself, with an ashen face and quaking with fear. Glancing in the direction of her petrified eyes he saw a gauzy figure floating as if on a breeze yet the air was still. The figure was that of a man complete with tunic, breeches and cloak. The girl shuddered as Calvin gently reached out and touched her shoulder. "Come inside—I will handle this." Calvin's voice was calmer than he felt. Blue eyes stared at him and she quickly entered the suite Calvin had vacated. "You'll be safe in here." Calvin drew the door shut so that the girl would be shielded from the wispy figure in the hallway.

Calvin studied the figure from a distance. The light from the hall filtered through like light through a dusty pane of glass. The figure was suspended in the air by its own accord and it bobbed up and down gently. The ghostly apparition had not proceeded down the hall but remained suspended in front of a door on the right. The ghost moved in a manner that seemed to be motioning Calvin to follow him, so with hesitant steps Calvin started down the hall, slowly and cautiously towards what lay in front of him. As he drew nearer the ghostly figure faded through the door. Calvin tried the handle and found the door open. With trepidation he pushed the door inward, toward the unknown, toward the blackness of the inner room.

Light from the hallway cast eerie shadows across sheet-draped furniture, cobwebs and dust. Calvin retreated to the hall for a candle, pulling one quickly from a gargoyle's hands before proceeding further into the room. Once again entering the room a ring of blackness edged the border of the candles glow, within the circle of light there was indeed sheet-draped furniture embroidered with spiders' intricate webs. Dust lay thick upon the objects in the room from years of neglect; piled deep upon their surfaces like snow upon the peaks of the highest mountains. Calvin half expected to find a skeleton sitting there, the original host to the ghost who led him, but that was not the case. He examined the room carefully. In one corner stood a desk uncovered except by the webs and dust upon it. Calvin noticed an envelope and picked it up sending a cloud of dust into the air making him sneeze. He waved his hand in front of his face to clear the dust away then opened the letter.

Inside was a handwritten letter in an old fashioned script. Upon closer examination it was more of a riddle than a letter, reading:

A spirit returns from whence he came
Return with music what remains
Spirit and bones will thus unite
When interlocked with the light

A ghoulish laughter can be heard
Howling grotesquely on the wings of birds
Shatter the glass that holds their voice
Thus will end the incessant noise

A goblin dangerous magic makes
Stay away from the crafted cage
Shield the eyes from the eagles stare
The cage will break with a single blare

A dragon's breath will sear your heart
Beware the temptress from the start
Set ablaze the midnight skies
The dragon's breath to no more rise

Calvin held the paper in his trembling hand. This was the quest and it was outlined for him, just as Logan had said it would be.

Faltering with the paper, light and staff he fumbled his way to the door. In the hallway Calvin pondered the words of the first few lines, carefully going over the writing again and again. Calvin realized that to get rid of the ghost he would need to find the music and Calvin was sure it was the music he had already heard.

The girl from the hall was still in his suite when he returned. A rosy hue splashed across her cheeks suggesting her fear had worn off. Calvin had no way of knowing how much time had elapsed for—as Eartheria had mentioned—it was the land of no time. There were no clocks or timepieces of any sort and no windows to speak of. The queen's chamber and the glen both existed in the twilight of the dawn shrouded by mist and masked from reality. The people here seemed to eat when they were hungry and sleep when they were tired. "Are you hungry?" Calvin asked and motioned to a chair as his stomach complained loudly, food completely forgotten in the haste of his rising.

"Yes, thank you," she replied. "Who are you?"

"I'm Calvin," he stated matter-of-factly. Calvin wasn't sure how to acquire the food he had just offered her, but he only knew that whenever he was hungry it was just there. Setting the staff down, he took the other seat opposite her and sure enough a table appeared laden with food in front of them, the table already set for two. "Please eat," he proclaimed, "we'll talk after." They dined on a sumptuous meal of herbed chicken with boiled red potatoes, mixed greens and grilled vegetables. Silence permeated the air between them, each one studying the other with unabashed interest. Calvin poured hot tea for them to accompany a variety of delicate desserts, and then they collected their thoughts and delved into the events of the day.

"I am Mira," the girl declared timidly. "You are not from here are you?"

"No I am from…" Calvin hesitated, "another place far away from here. I have come on a long journey masked with a mystery, one that I hope you might be able to help me with. The ghost that you saw is harmless other than the fright that he induces. He is a wandering apparition that I think I can bring to peace so that his bones and spirit will forever rest, but I need to find a girl, the one who played a flute this morning. Do you know her?" Calvin looked at Mira as she pondered what he had said.

A look of deep concentration crossed Mira's face as she considered Calvin's question, "Airia perhaps—I am not sure—but how do you know her?"

"I heard her playing this morning, a hauntingly beautiful melody, a song that touched my spirit. I followed the sound until I ventured upon a circular room with tall narrow windows with seats in them. She was sitting there playing but stopped soon after I walked in. I think she was embarrassed by my being there for she left quickly." Calvin frowned. "I do not know how to find my way back to that room or even if she will be there."

"I will help you," Mira quipped. "I owe you that much for your bravery in the corridor. The way is not too far and I am familiar with it. If you are with me, I will not be afraid."

Mira gave Calvin a weak smile. "We will start after you have rested, you seem tired, it has been a long day. I will come for you here." With that she rose to leave, part way to the door she turned "Not all that you see is real, look around the curtains." With that quizzical phrase she was gone.

Calvin moved about his suite from room to room, settling in and preparing for rest. It had indeed been a long day, although it did not seem so at the time. Upon waking he had followed the ghost into the strange room. He had searched it thoroughly but had it taken so long that he needed to rest? He bathed in the warm waters of his bathroom pool basking in the wildness of the room. The waterfall fell gently about his shoulders and fragrant flowers filled the air with a soft perfume. The water lulled him and he realized that he was indeed tired once again, he retreated to his bed where he found billowing softness in the layers of pillows there. He fell into bed and was asleep almost instantly. Not a restful sleep for again dreams riddled his sub-conscience spirit, the same as before, and he struggled, tossing and turning, fighting the shadows of his dreams.

Like before he awoke to the hauntingly beautiful melody that he had remembered. Caught up in the song he quickly dressed in a soft tunic of light blue and pants of blue the color of the deepest ocean. The cloak that he swung over one shoulder resembled cobalt, grabbing his staff he headed into the outer room. A soft knock sounded moments later at his door and Mira stood there dressed in a long velvet cloak of rose. "Are you ready?" she asked. Calvin nodded and they headed quickly down many passageways, Mira leading the way through the twisting maze until again they reached the circular room. Calvin looked at the windows, this time remembering what Mira had said, *"Not all that you see is real, look around the curtains."*

As Mira had predicted the windows were not real, they did not look out on beautiful hills with elegant flowing waterfalls, but instead it was as if a curtain was drawn upon a beautiful painting making it look real. Calvin wondered how much of what he saw was real and what was an illusion. Slowly they entered the room; startled Airia looked up and stopped playing. She looked as if to bolt from the room again, but seeing Mira she hesitated.

"Mira?"

"Yes Airia, I have brought a friend with me. He saved me from an apparition in the corridor and he needs your help if you are willing."

Airia looked at Calvin and considered what Mira had said. "What do you want of me?" she asked him.

"I want you to play for me, not here, but in another spot, one not as lovely as this one is but it is a journey. Will you help me?"

"But why? What will my playing hope to bring?"

"Peace to a wandering spirit, a fusing of spirit with bone, eternal rest to his being." Calvin looked determined. "The way is not too difficult, just long and cold. Mira could accompany us if she is willing—if you prefer. I do not think the journey to be dangerous." Calvin looked at both of them; they looked at each other.

"I will help you, but I think Mira should stay here in case we are gone too long she will know to bring help. Tell us exactly where we will go and what must be done so that she is as informed as I in the event she needs to look for us." Airia seemed set by her decision so Calvin related all that he knew and hoped that he was accurate in his summation. "I need help locating the entrance to the corridor by which I came, do you know it?"

Airia nodded in affirmation. "We will go right away, are you prepared?"

"After breakfast will be soon enough," he stated, "we should eat for we do not know how long we may be delayed. I have a suite, Mira can show you the way when you are ready, dress warm." Calvin was concerned but not overly; of the pieces of the quest he had been given this one seemed to be the safest and the only one of which he thought he knew what to do.

They separated paths to prepare for the journey, Calvin finding his way somehow back to his suite. Over-laden with food a table stood ready waiting for him and to his amazement a pouch that he could strap about his waist for additional food to take on his adventure. A deep velvet ebony black cloak with golden threads entwined in an intricate pattern was draped across one of the chairs. It was heavier than the one he wore and lined with shimmering satin. He took off the cobalt cape and carefully hung it in the armoire of his bedroom then proceeded to sit at the table of food and consume his fill. He put some things he thought would transport well in the pouch, apples, bacon strips that he carefully wrapped in a napkin, biscuits and hard-boiled eggs. "I need a thermos for tea," he thought out loud. Calvin looked around and found what looked like a horn with a cork in the end and a strap fastened to it. "Hmmm, this will do," he again stated aloud and filled it quickly. Just as he was finishing a knock sounded on the door. Calvin knew before he opened it that he would find Mira and Airia on the other side.

"Wonderful, are you ready to go?" he asked, the excitement filtering into his voice. They nodded in agreement.

"I will travel with you to the passage then I will return to wait for you here, if that is acceptable." Mira noted and Calvin nodded his head in agreement.

"That will be fine," he said. "How can I explain when we will be back? There is no time here?" Calvin suddenly felt uneasy, "I don't even know if it is morning or not—I have just been going about my days as if the time was still turning in my world, sleeping when I have been tired and eating when I have been hungry." His anxiety spilled out to the two girls.

"Do not be distraught for it is what we all do. I will know when it has been too long and seek assistance," Mira stated resolutely. "You shall become familiar with it as we are and learn to accept it."

"I do not hope to be here that long," Calvin returned. "I must finish this quest as quickly as possible and return to the place I am from." His courage and determination returning he exclaimed, "Let's go!"

The three acquaintances set off down the corridor, twisting and turning from one hallway to another. They walked at a good pace, but not so quickly that they would tire easily. As they passed doorways

Airia would remark about the rooms beyond. The kitchens, the den, the library, classrooms, on and on but Calvin's mind was preoccupied with the quest and just what he needed to accomplish. Mira and Airia noticed his distraction and quickly delved into a conversation of their own. Their lilting laughter reverberated from the walls and echoed down the hall. They seemed to hit it off beautifully and quickly became close friends.

When they reached the room with the dais Calvin somewhat knew where he was. He glanced at the girls and smiled at their newly found camaraderie. He reached out and touched the furniture in the room, one by one as they passed by, still awed by the beauty of the craftsmanship. The room was well lit even in the vast space it occupied and there was nothing that foretold of the adventure to come. Finally they stopped near the entrance to the passageway back to the graves.

Chapter 6

The way had been longer than he had remembered, but then he was still in shock when he had ventured through the first time. Compared to the hallways of the living quarters the passage was long, narrow, cold, and much darker giving rise to a foreboding of danger lurking in the shadows. Airia, Mira and Calvin bade each other farewell. Airia and Calvin continued forward into the corridor, waving to Mira until she resembled only a fleck in the distance. The gargoyles' eyes seemed to watch them eerily from the walls as they passed by under their flickering lit candles and Calvin's neck began to prickle once again. Instinctively Calvin's muscles twitched and he began to hurry, faster than they were already going, almost in a run.

The journey down was much quicker and less strenuous than the way up had been, just from gravity and their momentum. It was still some time before they found themselves standing in front of the tombs with the shrine of candles and odd plaques before them. "This place gives me the chills… " Airia shuddered.

"Yeah, me too!" Calvin motioned Airia to the kneeler. "You may sit there." Calvin watched as she pulled her flute from her cape then, when she appeared ready, asked her to begin to play.

"What should I play?" she asked him.

"The same song you played the first time I met you," he replied and she nodded. She knelt on the kneeler, situated her skirts then as she picked up the flute the haunting melody began to fill the air, in the silence of the underground room the music swelled. The volume increased into a crescendo of sound that reached far into the depths of the passageway and beyond.

Calvin watched as not one but several gauzy figures began their lisping cadence down the passage, swaying gently in an eerie dance of death. There was no breeze to carry them as they performed their unearthly dance. The spirits were not as defined as the figure in the hall had been yet they were distinguishable as persons with limbs and hands. The apparitions eased into the room, slowly as if they were part of a funeral dirge, inch by inch carrying a heavy load. When they were within the room they encircled the space each touching the ghostly hand of the other, still swaying in a rhythm of their own. Airia had closed her eyes engrossed in the melody that she played; she neither saw nor felt the ghostly presence. Calvin replayed the lines of the letter in his head:

A spirit returns from whence he came
Return with music what remains
Spirit and bones will thus unite
When interlocked with the light

What was the light? Calvin looked around, why hadn't he thought about that part before?

An abundance of candles were ensconced in glass about the kneeler. Although the candles blazed brightly Calvin was certain that the light in the letter was not referring to the candles. The symbols on the walls, ancient runes that spoke a forgotten language seemed to call out to him and Calvin studied them. Carefully he perused the plaques upon the walls, studying them intently when suddenly Calvin was filled with a sense of incredulity; he knelt beside Airia on the kneeler with the staff in his hands. On the floor in front of him was an indentation round about the size of the bottom of the staff. He fit the staff in the impression while the music continued to play and twisted the staff in a circular fashion until—at one particular point—the staff caught the light of the candles. Light erupted in slivers from the prism of the crystal on the staff, sending light in every direction. As the light caught on the wispy figures a rumbling noise could be heard. Both Calvin and Airia looked up and what they saw nearly made Airia faint, but Calvin urged her quickly to keep playing. The tombs in the walls crumbled open and bones rose stealthily from within, each skeletal remain moving to the position of its ghostly counterpart. As the bones and spirits united they bowed and disappeared, one by one until only one remained—the one from the hallway.

"You have come unto the light with a melody of the spirit, from this point hence you will call upon the light without the aid of the outside world, and you shall be called wizard." The ghostly wail sent shivers up Calvin's spine but the figure did not remain nor did he regale any further prophesy, he simply dissolved to join his ancestors in the tombs from whence they came. The walls of the tombs seemed to pull together as if the ghostly hands reached forth to pull the clumps of clay back into place and in a matter of minutes no one would have guessed what had just taken place. The walls once again solidly held together—appearing as they had once been.

Airia looked up, her eyes round with wonder. She looked around the room and shuddered then she looked at Calvin "Wizard? You are the wizard of the prophecy?"

Calvin looked at Airia perplexed. "I don't know what he was talking about, I have a quest to complete, that is all. A wizard would know magic and I know nothing of the kind." Airia continued to stare at him and Calvin began to feel uneasy. "Come let us head back, it has taken longer then I had hoped. We shall eat along the way." Calvin handed Airia an apple and they started back in silence. The uneasy feeling that Calvin had would not go away; he was unaware of the dangers that lurked around the corners for his mind was on the message the ghost had relayed.

Further along the passage Airia skipped lightly in front of Calvin. "A great wizard, I can't believe it."

Calvin scowled, "Leave me be, I told you I am nothing of the kind." A small smile twitched at the corners of his mouth at her antics. The amusement was short lived for as Airia skipped around the next bend she screamed, an earth shattering, heart wrenching scream, then disappeared.

Calvin's heart raced as he rounded the bend there was nothing there, not Airia, nothing but the gargoyles and candles upon the wall. He looked desperately a bit further on then backtracked to where she had been. He felt the walls but they were solid as the rock they were made of, the floor smooth and undisturbed. He looked for some sort of trigger or latch that would have tripped a door but found nothing.

Panic was beginning to set in.

Calvin closed his eyes and breathed, deeply trying to focus on the event just moments before, exactly what happened, and though he replayed the scene time and time again he came up with the same conclusion, nothing. He marked the spot as best he could so that he would know where to come to then headed back quickly, determination driving him.

The trip back to the castle, if you could call it that, was dismal. Calvin had the distinct impression he was being watched but each time he turned there was no one there. The all too familiar prickle ran down his neck and each time he flinched in response, but as to what caused it Calvin had no clue. The stairway up seemed steeper and longer than before and there was little comfort when he reached the top. He had to find her, there had to be something in the passage, but he would need better light and more food for he would not leave the passage again until he found her—if he found her.

Calvin's feet dragged across the granite floor, weighing heavy like the burden on his soul. Airia had been a wonderful companion to journey with and her haunting music even now filled him. He needed to hurry to get the supplies he would need and go back to look for her but he was zapped of energy, drained by the magnitude of the task before him. If only he knew how things materialized and disappeared he might know where to begin—but as it were he did not and so felt helplessly lost. Deep concentration on his thoughts precluded him from noting where he was until a sudden noise startled him and he found himself standing in front of the door to his suite, the noise coming from within.

Calvin entered to find Mira crying softly upon the sofa. "What is it? What is wrong?" Calvin asked, hurrying toward her.

"I know... " she faltered, "I know what happened in the corridor, she is gone isn't she." *How could she know?* Calvin wondered. "I saw her, in...in a dream. Oh it was terrible." Mira threw her face in her hands and wept. Calvin looked at her, calmly turning her chin towards him.

"She disappeared in the corridor, right in front of me, but I am going to find her. I came back to get supplies that I need. There was not enough light and I did not have enough food to continue my search for her. I am going straight back and I will find her, do you understand?"

Mira looked up tears in her eyes "I want to—to come with you," she hiccupped in a faltering voice.

"NO!" Calvin's harsh shout did not give her room to argue. "I have lost one person whom I could call friend I will not lose another. I must go alone for I do not know where I might wind up or what I might face. I only know that I will not return until I find her."

Mira looked in his eyes and knew that no argument she could make would change his mind. He was determined in his mission and no one or no thing was going to stop him.

"I'll help you get ready then." she replied her breath still ragged from crying. Calvin reviewed the list of items he felt he should have with him to improve his chances of finding Airia and Mira hurried quickly to find the things he said he would need. Once secured and carefully placed in a sack that he could sling across his back he set out once more, saying his goodbyes to Mira with tears in her eyes, then quickly headed down the corridor once more.

The trip was basically uneventful except for this nagging feeling he was being watched and the interminable prickle that ran down his neck. The pace he kept was brisk, almost a run in places, to reach the place he had marked. The search had already been delayed by his need for supplies there could be no further dalliance for his part. He looked about the floor with sharp eyes for the marker he had left. Finding it he knelt, laying the staff upon the floor and removed the sack from his back. He took a lantern out of the sack and struggled with a flint to light it. The light was slightly brighter than the candles and he was able to see the walls more clearly than before. The rune symbols marked the walls on either side but he could not read them to know what they might have said. A gargoyle sconce held a candle up in front of its face like the others that lined the corridor. Calvin looked at the gargoyle closely; perhaps the candle was some sort of catch that would make something move. He tried pulling the candle up, pulling it forward, pushing backwards and even pushing it down but to no avail. While he was concentrating on the candle he flinched, he thought he saw the gargoyles eyes move, but when he blinked and looked again they were the same as always.

Calvin felt the surface of all the stones carefully, the cold surface sending shivers down his spine, nothing moved. The sensation of being watched was very strong. Calvin picked up the staff, his sense of security. He looked at the wood carefully for on the twisted surface there were runes as well. He concentrated on the runes, those on the staff and those on the wall until a pair was present one on each. He called to mind what the ghostly apparition had said, *"You have come unto the light with a melody of the spirit, from this point hence you will call upon the light without the aid of the outside world, you shall be called wizard."*

Calvin concentrated on the crystal at the end of the staff, aligning the runes on the staff with the wall and slowly he began to hum the melody that Airia had played. He let his mind drift to the image of Airia, to the melody she played, that he now hummed, focusing all his energy on her; what she looked like, her voice, her song—his vision blurred.

"Calvin!" Airia shrieked. He shook his head vigorously and looked before him. Standing in front of him was Airia, beaming happily, not in the corridor for instead of Airia coming to him, he had gone to her. At that moment he did not care, for together they might be able to solve the mystery, she was alive and safe, safer now that they were together. Airia threw her arms around Calvin in a hold that nearly choked away his breath.

"Airia, what happened?" Calvin asked quizzically pulling back from her enough to let some air into his lungs.

"The gargoyles, they're alive."

"The…what?" Calvin couldn't phrase a response so taken aback by what she just said.

"The gargoyles, they're alive," she repeated then continued. "One of them snatched me from the corridor and brought me to this place. We seemed to go through the walls; it was so dark I could not see."

The prickling sensation started again at the back of his neck and Calvin finally knew the trigger, gargoyles. They had indeed been watching them and he felt stupid not to have realized that, he had felt their eyes boring into them, had thought he saw them move. How could he not have known they were a danger? There was nothing in the quest that addressed the gargoyles and Calvin had no idea where to begin; he only knew that they would need to leave the place they were in. Calvin's thoughts rambled in his mind as he looked about their surroundings.

Chapter 7

The room in which they were standing was dark and dank, similar to the cellar in his home, with moisture on the floors making them spongy. The air hung heavily and reeked of rotting wood making the air musty and stale. The unpleasantness of his surroundings made Calvin shudder but the companionship he now had lifted his spirits and he remained upbeat and positive.

"Do you know where we are?" he asked Airia.

"No, it is a place foreign to me. I have looked for a way out, but cannot see to find one." Airia's vision roamed around the room.

"The lantern I have went out when I shifted locations, if I can get it going again we will have the light that we need. The pack that I had of supplies however is not with me and I do not have a lighter." Calvin frowned perplexed.

"Use your staff, Calvin," Airia urged. "It is your source of power I am certain of it. Use it like you did to come here, like you did to ease the spirits; somehow it is connected to you."

"But how? I don't know how anything works here. I don't know how the staff works."

"Concentrate, just concentrate," Airia replied gently. Calvin screwed up his face in concentration focusing on the light. "You're trying too hard," Airia murmured softly.

Calvin continued to focus, only this time he tried to ease his mind to let go of all the other thoughts running through it. He envisioned light, a bright light that would cast a white glow around the room, he thought of the lantern, the wick, the fuel contained within to light the fire. For several long moments he continued until he actually felt warmth, a glow building, not in the lantern which he held but in the staff. The crystal on the end of the staff glowed brightly as if the sun was shining from within the faceted face of its surface. Calvin could not look directly at the blazing surface for the brightness blinded him. Setting the lantern on the floor he pointed the staff at the wick in its center and a small spark began to glow, the wick caught the delicate flicker and erupted into a steady flame. Calvin lit the candle not for the need of more light but more accurately because he did not know how long the staff would remain lit and he wanted an assurance of light.

The room was now flooded with a bright light that revealed even the smallest of corners. The floors were indeed covered in water, not deep but enough that the floor was saturated and small puddles remained on the surface. A slimy mold clung to rotting rafters that rose above them holding back the soil from above and attributed to the stench of decay within the room. A space no larger than a few feet weaved above the dirt walls and between the beams supporting some sort of floor above it. Calvin put the light up next to the space and peered intently inside. "I think I can crawl through this. Who knows where it leads to, but there has to be some way out."

"I'm going with you," Airia stated, grimacing at the thought of what might lurk within the space. "I'm definitely not being left behind."

"The way will not be pleasant," Calvin said, "but I could not ask you to remain. We will go together, who knows what we will face." Calvin lifted Airia up to the edge of the opening. "Grab the edge slightly and pull yourself in a little until I climb up."

He handed her the lantern but the staff he retained clutched in his grasp, afraid that if he let it go the bright light would fade away. Awkwardly he managed to get a handhold and jumped off the floor and swung his legs toward the opening trying to get his feet up on the ledge. Airia reached out quickly as one foot barely found the edge and held his ankle firmly as he used the staff as a sort of pry bar to push himself the rest of the way onto the ledge, then he carefully started crawling towards the interior. "Follow me but be careful," he whispered to Airia.

Cautiously they made their way forward, painstakingly slow as they had to stop every couple of paces to move the lantern forward.

The staff remained bright and cast an eerie shadow about the dirt, beams and spiders' webs that adorned the space, the spiders taking refuge in the corners. Occasionally a mouse would race across their path and Airia had all she could do to stifle a scream. They could not see the path they had traversed behind them, before them stretched what seemed like an endless path of nothing but the same. There was no end to the space in front of them, no openings, no light from the outside land.

"Airia, I want to try something," Calvin said, his face creased in an expression of puzzlement. "When I was looking for you I concentrated on you, entirely on you and your music and suddenly I was with you. I had hoped I would somehow draw you to me but it worked in reverse. Now I'm going to try the same thing, only this time concentrating on the Glen, a place I visited once before, and Logan, a friend. I don't know how it works exactly but with luck we will find ourselves in the Glen. You will need to hold on to me for I think it is the contact with the staff that permits the shift through space and I don't know about you but I want to get out of here as quickly as we can, I cannot see any other way."

Airia didn't answer, she just nodded her head in agreement. They were covered in muddy muck, there were bugs and spiders everywhere, which, coupled with the occasional mouse was more than a lady could bear. She inched forward and wrapped her arms about Calvin's waist then let him concentrate; Calvin on the other hand had not expected her arms about his waist to be such a distraction and he found the concentration more difficult than he had imagined. He concentrated fully on the Glen, of Logan, of the cabin, of the waterfall and every other detail he could remember. Slowly the image of the crawl space faded from his vision and the image of the Glen replaced it, the sweet smell of the misty morning permeated the air.

"What has happened? Are you alright?" Logan rushed from the cottage towards the two weary travelers, fear and concern crossing his wrinkled face. "Come inside!" he gestured to Calvin towards the cottage and cradled one of Airia's arms within his, urging them forward to the warm dry interior.

"We are fine," Calvin replied, "just dirty and hungry. After we are clean we shall tell you our tale, you will find it most interesting."

Logan ushered Airia to a washstand in the corner and pulled a curtain around it. "Come," he said to Calvin, "give her some privacy." They drew out the door and down toward the water's edge where the water from the falls swirled gently around the colorful array of flowers that swept up in the midst of moss and the clear liquid. Calvin bent over, pulling his boots from his feet and leaned over the water, quickly swiping at the mud caked upon his face, arms, and hands, looking at Logan he shrugged then plunged into the icy cold cleansing himself from head to toe. The cape about him sagged with the weight of the water pulling him downward into the depths. Quickly Calvin undid the fastenings then pulled with lean, muscular arms toward the surface dragging the cloak behind him. He emerged from the water, skin pink from the chill, and wrung out the cloak as best he could. There was not much he could do about his tunic and breeches without taking them off so he left them as they were.

"I'll leave these in the sun to dry," Calvin exclaimed as he picked up his boots and strolled towards the cottage. He set the boots on the porch then settled down beside them.

Moments later the door opened and Airia stood looking timidly out from behind. "You can come in now," she said and drew the door inward allowing the others to enter. Calvin hung his cloak by the fire, hoping it was not ruined from the water, but the water was better than the mud that had preceded it. He dripped water onto the floor and little puddles remained where he had been standing. He edged toward the fire where Airia had placed a pot of water on the hearth to boil for tea. She had also rummaged together biscuits and cheese to stave off the hunger that they both felt.

Logan set about busily preparing a meal as they munched on the bits Airia had found. "Tell me what happened?" he asked, his curiosity driving him mad.

Airia began the tale telling from her side while Calvin filled in the pieces and related the rest. Logan's eyes were wide with shock and anxiety as they unraveled the threads of the story, he sighed more than once, and caught his breath at times, but then relief rushed over him as the story ended at the Glen. "There is nothing to be done about the gargoyles. Their existence has always been, it is a mystery with no end," Logan told them. "They are solitary creatures that exist in their stony state except occasionally when some outside force interferes with them. Perhaps they sensed the magic of your staff; magical creatures can often do mysterious things."

They sat about sharing the pieces of the adventure and dining on the simple stew Logan had made to go with the biscuits and cheese Airia had found. They sat for a long time until their yawns gave way that they were exhausted. "You will spend the night," Logan said as a matter of fact. "You look weary still and there is room." Logan led them to separate rooms in the cottage, which was bigger than it appeared. The rooms were small, clean and quaint. Calvin's head barely touched the pillow before he was asleep.

The morning dawned with the same mist shrouding the cottage and all that surrounded it. The room where Calvin slept was cold the chill making him shiver. He jumped from the bed and nearly jumped back into it at the briskness of the floor beneath his feet but instead he hurried out the door into the front room where the hearth blazed brightly and Logan was busily preparing a breakfast feast. "You look well!" he exclaimed as he surveyed Calvin's appearance. "Would you like some tea?"

"Yes, thank you," he murmured hiding his yawn behind his hand, "I would love some." He stood on the rug before the hearth with his hands outstretched towards the warmth of the fire, he would have put his feet out too except he thought he would follow some decorum. After drawing the warmth so that the rest of his body was no longer chilled he strode across the room to the door. "I'm just going to grab my boots," he chimed. He popped the door open and quickly walked to where his boots rested. Calvin brushed them with the flat of his hands until they did not look so unsightly then carried them back inside. He set them near the fire to warm and continued his stance upon the rug, unwilling to give up the warmth of the fire just yet.

"Here, drink this. It will warm you up some. The heat doesn't go to the back rooms—I'm sorry about that," Logan apologized.

"That is quite all right, I slept comfortably and well. It was not until rising that I noticed the chill. I will be fine momentarily." Calvin brushed off the apology as none was needed.

They stood in silence for a time each sipping a cup of hot tea and trying to shake the web of sleep from their eyes. After a short time Airia entered the room looking more cheerful then the other two. "What's the matter with you two? You look like you've been out all night." She laughed at the look they gave her.

"Perhaps I'll let you fend for your own breakfast?" Logan retorted with a slight grin pulling at the corners of his mouth.

"Oh, I'm sorry I did not mean to offend you." Airia quickly proffered but she caught the hint of the grin and they all chuckled in the dim morning light. They ate heartily of the feast Logan had prepared. There was sausage, bacon, eggs, biscuits, pancakes and fresh fruit of several varieties. When they were finished they pushed back their chairs and sighed contentedly.

"Would you like to see some of the Glen this morning?" Logan asked. "I have to collect some herbs and things and could show you about if you don't mind the jaunt."

"That would be wonderful!" Calvin exclaimed and Airia nodded her head in agreement.

They dressed for the weather pulling on warmed boots and heavy cloaks. Calvin found his to be in perfect condition after drying before the hearth through the night. Logan handed them shallow baskets for collecting the herbs and they all started the trek into the heart of the Glen. The air though misty was fragrant and sweet, the scent of moisture mixing it into an aromatic cloud of gentle perfume. The dew on the ground dampened their boots on the outside, but did not yet soak them through. A narrow path wound between rocks, over humps and culminated in a clearing surrounded by majestic trees. The sun shone through the mist in patches catching the droplets within the clouds and casting a rainbow across the clearing.

Calvin and Airia looked at the rainbow in awe, both holding their breath briefly at the exquisite site before them. "Come it is not much farther," Logan stated as they continued to plod forward towards the end of the rainbow. Beneath the colorful arch was a patch of bright green, succulent and tender. Logan bent down and carefully harvested a few clumps and placed them in a basket. A little way further along was a patch of petite pale blue flowers with delicate stems and Logan again bent down carefully cutting off the slender stalks and placing some in the basket. They continued in this fashion until all the baskets were full, a mosaic of color on the brown reed bins. They talked animatedly about all different things and soon found that it was time to head back.

Logan pointed out the different areas of the Glen with a wealth of knowledge of what it contained; his love for the Glen evident as he swelled with pride as he talked of the special place. Suddenly, without warning a horrible shriek pierced the air and the shadow of an unseen beast wafted through the air across the stillness of the glen. "Run," Logan yelled as he swiftly ran towards the other end of the Glen and the cottage. Airia and Calvin ran quickly and overtook the old man. They grabbed his arms in an attempt to move him faster, but the old man could only move so fast. "Go," he shouted at them and pointed toward the cottage giving them a shove. They continued on without him glancing back to make certain he did not collapse along the way. From the cottage porch they could see him stumble and Calvin raced back to help him. The shadow was coming once again in their direction and the shrieking had not subsided since it began. Calvin looked up, staff in hand, ready to do battle, but all they could see was the shadow, the beast itself remained unseen. Faltering they managed to get to the porch, the old man gasping for breath and Calvin fighting to help him inside. Airia opened the door and stood ready as the two of them stumbled over the threshold then she slammed the door keeping the beast outside.

"What was that?" Calvin gasped.

Logan looked at him, fear written in every line of his wrinkled face. "Ghouls" was all he could say then he collapsed in a heap on the floor. Calvin and Airia struggled to pick the old man up and laid him on the soft bed in the corner, his soft eyes fluttered to look at them for only a moment then they closed once again.

"He is breathing," Calvin relayed to Airia whose concern overwhelmed her, "he needs rest, that is all." Airia receded to the far corner of the room and rummaged about finding what she needed to make a broth while the sound of the ghoul's incessant shrieking made them cringe. The old man slept a long time, tossing in fits upon the mattress, exhausted from the terror of the day. Calvin and Airia both stood vigil beside him afraid to leave his side until he was awake. When he awoke Airia hurried for some broth, putting it in a mug so it would be easier to drink and handed it to Logan. He drank slowly, letting the warm liquid flow into his mouth, savoring the flavor and reviving the stress torn body of old age.

"They are gone?" he asked fearfully.

"Yes, they have left but who knows when they will return. They are the ones from my dream, I am certain of it, the dream I had when first I arrived. What are they really?" Calvin needed to know what it was he was dealing with, maybe then he would have a solution.

"They are ghouls, undead, unearthly creatures that wander the lands. They scream with the voices of thousands of dead or more and can make a man go mad, insane from the horror they unfold. They can instill nightmares into your soul as if you had really lived it, haunting you until you become only the shell of a man." Logan shuddered and closed his eyes trying to erase the thoughts from his mind, but it was not that simple and he continued. "On wings of eagles it is said they fly but they are not truly eagles, the wings that carry them are their own formed from souls gone mad and bound by magic. Legend tells of a glass sphere entombed in a cavern on the far side of the glen, through the deep forest, but the forest is haunted, full of mystical beasts and the fear of the ghouls has kept any traveler from discovering the location. As it is legend—one cannot tell if it is true, only know this, most legends hint of a truth that is sometimes exaggerated."

Airia sat stiffly on the edge of the bed, fear obviously riveting her where she was. Calvin reached out and gently took her hand. "It will be all right; you will go back to the castle and remain there. I will go on with the quest, it is mine to complete, not yours."

"You cannot go alone it is too dangerous and you do not know the ways of this land." Airia was distraught.

"He will not be alone my dear lady," Logan murmured, "I will be with him. Old I may be, but I know the lay of this land and am familiar with most of the creatures. Together we may stand a chance, alone neither of us would survive."

"Ohhh..." Airia inhaled sharply at the last comment Logan had made, her eyes wide with unconcealed terror.

"Shhh..." he said, patting her knee, "Calvin is right, it will be all right."

Logan rose from the bed and hobbled to a cabinet, his back to the others he began to mix something together. "Here drink this, it will bring you peace," he stated. He handed Airia a small glass of a dubious looking mixture, she furrowed her brow at the brew and looked hesitantly at Logan. "Drink," he said in more of a command than a suggestion. She put the glass to her lips and drank quickly, finding the concoction to be much better tasting than it looked. "Now rest," he said and helped her to lie on the bed he had vacated.

Logan motioned Calvin to the door. Once on the porch outside he confided in Calvin. "The draught I gave her is a sedative, she will rest peacefully but she will also awaken in her home. She will think she has had a dream and she will not remember most of what has happened, at least not until she is able to face it."

"So, she will not be on the bed when we return inside?" Calvin glanced at the door.

"No, it is better this way." Logan was wise both in knowledge and years. Calvin accepted this and let his thoughts wander to the quest he had read. It seemed ages ago that he had found the letter and he had to replay the lines several times in his head before he focused on the part they had to deal with.

A ghoulish laughter can be heard
Howling grotesquely on the wings of birds
Shatter the glass that holds their voice
Thus will end the incessant noise

The letter made it all seem so simple. Calvin knew that it was not, Logan knew that it was not and together they would face the unknown dangers. Calvin needed to learn as much from Logan as he could before they ventured on the journey, and they needed to start very soon. Logan motioned to the door and they returned inside, Airia had vanished to her home where she belonged, the cottage seemed somehow empty even though the place was still filled with all the things Logan collected and stored. She had fit in here.

Calvin and Logan talked long and in depth about the journey. Logan pointed at plants and herbs and explained the properties that they possessed. There was sneeze weed particularly helpful in allergy attacks, dermatite excellent for healing skin, hemafluke to aid in stopping profuse bleeding, temper twigs for calming and so forth and so on. Logan showed Calvin how to make several different mixtures to get various results that they might need and—he showed Calvin how to make the calming tea. Thus the ancient secret was passed from the wise old healer to the young wizard assuring for the moment that the recipe would not be lost.

Chapter 8

The sacks they filled were heavy but not so much so that they could not carry them upon their backs. Calvin made sure to lighten Logan's load somewhat and took more of the things that Logan had set aside for them. They each had two smaller sacks to tie on their belts that contained herbs separated into tiny bundles. These Logan explained were special, of great healing properties among other things.

"Wear these," Logan said as he thrust an armful of clothes at Calvin. "They are more suitable for the woods and we will blend in." Calvin took the clothes and retreated to the back room to change. There were brown pants of soft leather, a tunic of a mossy green the material soft but foreign to him and a cloak also of brown but lined with fur for warmth, the edge rolled back around the opening. The clothes smelled of the outdoors, strong but not repugnant. Boots of sturdy leather that laced to his knees and a wide belt completed the wardrobe. Calvin hurriedly dressed then went in the outer room to attach the sacks. Calvin took the cord of the sacks and ran them through his belt, lacing them securely. The heavier sack he slung upon his back and he shifted his weight to accommodate the additional load. He looked at Logan who was similarly dressed and the two of them headed off, Calvin's staff secured in his hand.

The way was not cheerful like their previous trek, but rather both men were serious and thoughtful, taking care not to make too much noise. The path across the Glen was easy to follow and meandered aimlessly in a casual manner. At the forest edge however the path was obscure to non existent. The dense canopy masked the way beneath in a veil of darkness. The trees were old and large in circumference, creating huge pillars that supported the canopy above. There was little vegetation on the forest floor, scattered sprigs of green peaking from piles of dead and decaying leaves and limbs. The air hung heavy with the scent of mold from the dampness that clung to the decay.

About the forest there was a stillness and quiet as if even the animals were afraid of what lay inside the forest's edge. Calvin shivered and pulled the cloak closer about him. He drew the hood of the cloak up about his head and gripped the staff tighter in his hand. Logan caught Calvin's movements, glanced at him, then did the same as Calvin and pulled his cloak closer about him. A short ways into the forest they came to a narrow stream which crossed the path. "We'll rest here," Logan said and set his heavy pack upon the ground. Calvin could have gone further but realized the trip was hard for the old man, especially after the fright of the preceding day. There was water here so that they could replenish their supply and neither knew when the next opportunity to do that would arise. Logan began making a fire from debris scattered around them. He placed a small pot that he retrieved from his pack onto the fire and began to brew his wonderful tea. The scent rose from the pot and immediately eased some of the tension the two felt.

Calvin broke the silence and nearly jumped from how loud his voice seemed in the otherwise silent place, "Logan, do you have any idea how far we might travel? These woods look like they go on forever."

Logan looked about and shrugged. "Maybe two or three days, maybe more, I'm not sure. I have not needed to come this far nor has anyone returned that did. With luck it will be shorter than not." Logan sighed. "An old legend talks of the caverns and of the dangers that lurk within the forest surrounding it, but the legend is old, and we do not know if it is valid. I have some parchment and will try to map the way that we go so that a written legacy will follow us should we return." Calvin and Logan talked about other things, of the herbs, the land and everything that they might encounter then they both settled into their cloaks and they stretched out upon the ground for a restful night.

Calvin woke first, with a start, a slimy sensation weighing upon his legs. He sat upright with some difficulty and noted a strange vine entangled about his feet. The vines seemed to be sprouting up from the ground and were pulling his feet tightly towards the surface. He tried to claw the vines away but could not get a grasp on the slimy surface. He called to Logan who woke and rose quickly. Calvin's feet had disappeared below the surface of the ground as if they were stuck in the muck at the bottom of a swamp. Logan grabbed a blade he had used earlier in the day, working as quickly as he could he slashed at the vines entangling Calvin, the vines twisting and turning trying to latch onto Logan as well. By the time Logan had cleared the vines, Calvin was up to his knees in the ground below. Calvin clawed at the ground digging his legs out and Logan stood guard over the patch of vines ready to slash any stray strands that remained. "What was that thing?" Calvin asked brushing the dirt and slime from his pants.

"Quagenvines," Logan replied, breathing roughly from his morning fright. "It's a vine that pops up anywhere and sucks you downward turning the ground into a mucky quagmire like you would find in a swamp, hence the name. Nasty stuff and there is no way of knowing where it will crop up."

"Figures—" Calvin said, "I don't think this slime will dry off enough to wipe off either, any suggestions?"

Logan looked at the mess and thought for a moment. "Flour I think; it will thicken the stuff enough to scrape off at least. I'm sorry we don't have a change of clothes, but there is only so much one can carry." Logan reached in his pack and pulled out a sack of flour and together they dusted the slime that covered Calvin's pants, the white flour giving him a ghostly appearance. Calvin scraped the surface of his clothes with the blade that Logan had previously used, what remained gave Calvin the appearance of someone who had not washed in many months. Logan put a pot of tea on the fire and they sat down to eat cold biscuits and drank the warm tea. They stuffed their belongings back in their packs and set off towards the other end of the forest.

They had to cross the little stream on flat rocks that were scattered across it. The rocks were slippery in places from a greenish moss that clung to the sides. Logan's foot slipped into the water in a couple of places but he shook it off and continued on trying to keep up with Calvin and his brisk pace. The path wound about and frequently faded, making them look about for where it began again. They walked for quite a distance with the dense trees blocking the light, blanketing the forest in a cold darkness. After a time rocks appeared sporadically placed with large blobs of muck and mud interspersed in between. Roots and vines ran haphazardly among the rocky terrain, making the way difficult to navigate and often one or the other of them fell.

A small clearing seemed to mysteriously appear among the dense woods and the bright patch of sun sprinkling over a dusting of flowers left the travelers awe struck. They hurried into the clearing and found a small spring trickling up from a crevice by a large boulder in the middle of the clearing. They set down their packs and made camp, feeling the need of rest not only for their weary bones but for their spirits—the weight of their journey seeping into the edges of their existence and permeating the aura about them.

They slept soundly with only the slightest awareness of their surroundings. Well rested they rose and ate a light meal washed down as usual with a warm cup of tea. They packed their sacks once again and set out, on the diminished trail toward the unknown. A short while later they heard what sounded like grunting, deep, guttural, like a mad beast. They hid behind a large tree and listened intently, trying to locate the source of the sound. Calvin spotted the creature first, a massive pig like creature with long sharp tusks and knobby gnarly globs of thick tough skin colored a magenta red covering it. Smoke rose from its snout with every guttural growl. "A gnarly boar," Logan whispered. The gnarly boar stood between two boulders with the path leading squarely in between. There were high walls on either side, preventing the two travelers from skirting around the troublesome spot.

"What is provoking him?" Calvin asked Logan, noting the animal's obvious distress.

"Numnuts—" Logan replied, "venomous little creatures that bite savagely leaving a poison that numbs the body slowly until its prey drops, then they consume it." Calvin looked closely at the animals a distance in front of him. On the ground were smooth round creatures with vicious little mouths of sharp teeth. Small legs seemed to sprout from their sides and they furiously attacked the gnarly boar with a vengeance. "We've got to keep moving, when they get done with him they'll be looking for some other kind of sport and from the looks of this area, we're it." Logan's phrase gave Calvin a chill and they continued forward dodging behind trees wherever possible.

The beast roared, then stumbled and fell, right into the center of the path. The eyes glazed over and rolled back into his head. Calvin cringed at the sight. The numnuts barrage left little marks on the thick hide of the beast but other than that the beast was intact. The hide looked too tough for anything to penetrate, but the venom must have seeped inside. Calvin's vision focused on a fissure on the right side of the closest boulder. "Think you can squeeze through?" Calvin eyed Logan, then the fissure, mentally assessing the distance. "We won't have much time and it looks a little tight."

Logan glanced in the direction Calvin pointed. "I'll make it, I have to."

While the attention of the numnuts was on the boar Calvin and Logan dashed for the crack in the boulder. They were nearly there when the numnuts suddenly realized there was additional prey about. The numnuts sped across the distance and Calvin shoved Logan toward the crack with a huge effort. Logan managed through the crack in record time but as Calvin entered the crack a sharp pain lanced his ankle, he kicked wildly at his attacker but already he felt the effects of the venom taking hold. Calvin took the staff that he held firmly in his hand, pointed it at the numnuts and concentrated on obliterating the little beast. He focused his mind and suddenly the creature was gone. Calvin crawled forward through the crack, Logan pulling on his free hand, until he safely reached the other side. "Can you walk?" Logan asked with deep concern.

"No, it's my left leg; the venom is swarming up my leg like bees on a hive and with it a numbing sensation that is preventing me from feeling anything below the knee."

"Here," Logan said and helped Calvin to stand, "lean on me."

Together they managed to move from the boulder down a rocky path cut in the mountain, to a dusty patch of ground with a barren tree. Logan used the tree to prop Calvin up then quickly rummaged among his herbs, taking one out in a deep purple color with small bluish blooms dried upon the branches. He used his knife to crush the herb into a fine powder against one of the stones then mixed some water into it. Logan pulled Calvin's boot off and pushed the hem of his pants up to expose the wound. It was a small elliptical spot but there was no blood so to speak of. Logan scooped up some of the mixture he made with the blade of the knife and smeared it onto the wound. Then he bound the ankle with a small rag. "That should draw the venom out," he stated plainly. "Won't do any good to go gallivanting about on it though but we can hardly stay here."

Calvin looked at the first aid Logan had applied and gave a look of approval. "I'll be fine, for a while anyway. Let's get out of here before those things decide to come after us." Logan offered no complaint at that and he quickly shoved his stuff back in the bag and helping Calvin they continued on going slightly downhill at first, then upwards, the way becoming increasingly rough. Fragmented boulders and rocks lined the path with sharp jagged edges. They had to proceed carefully and Calvin's leg made the going slow.

Logan looked up and frantically half-carried, half-dragged, Calvin under a rock ledge, obscured behind a boulder not far from the tree they had recently left. The ghouls were back, the howling wails piercing the air around them. Rocks tumbled in a landslide of dust and ash. The two covered their ears with their hands and shrank back as far as they could. Calvin motioned for Logan to follow him and they inched their way along the ridge staying just out of sight of the ghouls. Before long the ghouls flew off leaving a blanketing silence that enveloped the area. Calvin and Logan continued on, both of them afraid that their ear drums had ruptured and they had gone completely deaf, but the crunch of their footsteps upon the fallen rocks assured them that their hearing was intact. They rambled on picking their way carefully over the debris strewn path and exerted more energy than anyone should have had to. After a fashion they had to stop, neither one of them up to any more travel for the day. The adventure had turned into a nightmare and exhausted they made camp and quickly fell asleep.

Morning brought the trials of the trail ahead. Jagged rocks jutted sharply into their path as it rose steeply for a time then leveled off, winding around the edge of the mountain. A deep cavern plummeted downward to the right as they moved toward the left on a narrow rocky ledge, rocks plunging off as they accidentally kicked them in their movement around the edge. A fine mist made the path slippery and treacherous. "Watch out," Calvin said as Logan slipped, his foot dangling from the edge of the path. Calvin helped Logan regain his footing. "Are you all right?"

Logan, breathing hard, looked down where he had almost tumbled. "Yeah—" he faltered, "I am now." The path twisted downward again giving them a slight reprieve before crumbling into a chasm that lead toward a distant cave. The way was overcome with sharp jagged rocks, their fragmented pieces skewed in different directions along with giant boulders too big to move.

The sight of the blackened entrance gave cause for great excitement to both Calvin and Logan, but the excitement was short lived once they started along the treacherous path. They crawled up and over and around and under and in between boulder after boulder until finally they reached the entrance. They were so exhausted by then that they were unable to even utter a small victory cry. Calvin's leg had begun to throb with a regular beat like a song on a drum, the venom wending its way back from where it had begun. Calvin rubbed his boot absently while he looked at the entrance. It was black inside, too dark to make out what lay closest to the entrance. A damp cold melted into the air outside creating a fine fog around the opening. Logan noted Calvin rubbing his leg. "Hurt much?"

"Not much," Calvin replied.

"Let me tend it anyway, while I have some light to work with," Logan replied. He set about making the salve once again, then pulled Calvin's boot off with a bit more difficulty then the first time. Calvin's ankle was swollen and an ugly black color swirled with purple around his leg, heat radiating from the spot where he had been bit. "Hmm, not good," Logan said.

Calvin bent forward to look at the spot and nearly gagged. He wasn't very good with injuries or illness and the sight of the grotesque swollen mass was more than he could stomach. Logan took his knife and said, "This will hurt a bit." He quickly lanced the wound on his ankle. He poured some water over the wound then let the air at it. While the wound was drying Logan began to build a fire and put a pot of water on it to boil. "Gotta clean it out son, sorry." Logan looked at Calvin sympathetically; Calvin nodded his teeth still clenched from the sting of the blade.

When the water was hot Logan scooped a cup out and added

different herbs into it. Then he soaked the rag in the water and placed it over the wound. Calvin yelped but then sighed after the initial shock of the heat against his swollen leg, his leg started to feel better almost immediately. Several more times Logan soaked the rag and placed it on Calvin's ankle until finally he was satisfied, then he scooped up the salve and smeared it liberally onto the wound and bound it up once again. "We'll camp here; tomorrow we'll enter the caves. We may not have another chance to rest for a while so we best make the most of it here. Enjoy the sun, after tomorrow we'll be confined to the darkness," Logan told Calvin as he began to work on their evening feast. Calvin looked at the sunshine then lay back and elevated his leg in the air and absorbed the wondrous rays. Before long Logan handed him a plate of herbed stew and warm biscuits, the meal was simple but delicious and filling. They topped it off with fresh fruit then sat around inhaling the fresh air and talking amiably of the journey they had. When their eyes became heavy the two lay down where they were and slept.

Waking refreshed the two travelers stretched and ate a simple breakfast of cold biscuits and fruit. From the first appearance the cave proved even blacker than it had looked when they finally ventured into it. Logan carried a torch he had made from the fire he had made the previous day. It glowed warmly, but the dank inner walls of the cave washed over them chilling them to the bone. Calvin and Logan both pulled the hoods of their cloaks up over their heads and pulled the front closed tightly about them, only the hand with the staff and the hand with the torch poking out into the dark about them. They followed the twisting cavern downward, stopping from time to time to scratch a mark into the wall or the floor so as not to lose their way. The air about them seemed to howl, not unlike the ghouls but not as loud. They journeyed a long way until at last they reached what appeared to be the floor of the cave. At the end of the cave was a huge waterfall, spilling out from what looked like solid rock, falling into the stream below. A mist hung in the air about the falls lending more moisture to the already soaked, underground interior. Logan walked forward and knelt by the spring. He scooped up a handful of water and tentatively brought it to his lips. "Mmm, good water," he said "tastes a bit like minerals, but at least it is drinkable. We had better fill our pouches." He took both of their pouches and replenished their stock rather pleased with the availability of the water. "Where do we go from here? It looks like the end of the line?" he murmured.

"We need more light," Calvin mumbled and held out his staff. He concentrated on the crystal at the end as he had before and thought as hard as he could about light, bright vibrant light. Before long the staff threw a brilliant light about the cave and with the aid of the light Logan and Calvin were able to note the narrow pathway that continued downward into the dark unknown. Stalactites and stalagmites cropped up and hung everywhere, drops of water trickling from the ends and dropping to the counterpart below. The air hung heavy with the minerals from the earth surrounding the narrow passage intertwined with the crisp coolness from being so far beneath the surface. The noise that they had heard continued vibrating between the walls.

The farther downward they proceeded, the louder the howl became. After what seemed like an eternity both men drew out of the narrow corridor into a large cavernous room, the sound there deafening. Calvin and Logan clapped their hands over their ears once again. In the center stood a pillar, upon which lay a large sphere. The sphere looked like ice, clear on the outside and a frosty bluish hue within. Calvin thought once more of the written quest.

A ghoulish laughter can be heard
Howling grotesquely on the wings of birds
Shatter the glass that holds their voice
Thus will end the incessant noise

Seemed simple enough, all he had to do was break the sphere, but that proved much more difficult than he would have imagined. Everything that he threw at the sphere just seemed to bounce off and clatter upon the rocks surrounding it. He tried to pick it up but it would not budge. Calvin took the staff he carried and slammed it against the side yet the sphere remained. Looking in the glass of the sphere Calvin thought that he saw the hideous ghoul staring back at him. The horrible, high-pitched noise resembled fingernails being raked down a chalkboard at times and Calvin was certain, that in itself would shatter nearly anything. He focused his thoughts of the noise on the staff and on the sphere in the center of the room before him. Logan covered his ears as Calvin continued to concentrate until suddenly the sphere cracked, then fragmented and finally shattered before them. As soon as the sphere broke, the ghoulish noises subsided. The hideous noise faded from existence into the realm of nothingness. They had beaten the second portion of the quest. Calvin and Logan did a sort of jig of happiness before starting up towards the entrance to the cavern.

"Logan, I would rather not go back the way we came, are you up for a little magic?" Calvin asked not wanting to venture back through the numnuts and quagenvines.

"What did you have in mind?" Logan asked, eyeing him suspiciously.

"Just hold onto the staff and I'll show you." Calvin quipped and before you could stop them both men disappeared from the cave and found themselves standing once more in the Glen.

Content to be home Logan threw his head back, breathed deeply then howled in joy. A huge grin spread upon his face and he said, "Come on I'll race you to the cottage." This time Calvin was certain the old man won.

The first thing Calvin did was to wash thoroughly from head to toe. His skin felt grungy after the long trip and days of being in the same clothes. He did not wait for water to warm but plunged clothes and all into the pool at the base of the waterfall, remembering beforehand to pull off his boots and cloak unlike his previous dip. He swam to the waterfall and let the water cascade over his head, then dove back into the water, savoring the feel. He pulled himself up on shore a while later letting the warm sun shine upon him and basked in the light and warmth. He closed his eyes for a moment and breathed a deep sigh, when he opened them again Airia and Mira were standing there, giggling.

Calvin looked at the pair and rolled over to stand, but before they noticed his movement he swiped them both into the pool where they sputtered and screamed more in delight than fright. They played for a time in the water splashing it back and forth and then floating lazily. Finally the trio pulled themselves up and lay in the sun to dry. The girls' dresses spread about them in huge sweeping circles to let the delicate fabric dry. Calvin regaled them with stories of his travels and both girls gasped when he hesitantly showed them his leg. "Oh,

Calvin, how can you stand the pain," they shuddered.

"It's nothing really, looks worse than it is" he replied modestly.

When they had dried, or nearly so, they moved to the cottage where Logan sat on the porch smiling at their antics. He had brewed his famous tea and prepared a huge feast. They ate heartily then Logan played them some music and they danced about with unabashed merriment until their eyes grew heavy with sleep. Calvin bid his old friend goodbye, with a girl on each arm he concentrated on his suite and before he could utter another sound they found themselves safely back in the posh interior of his rooms. The girls quickly said their good-byes and left Calvin to the quiet. The fires were lit and the candles burned brightly, remembering the dark cold of the cave Calvin left them as they were and fell into bed sleeping soundly.

Chapter 9

A knock on his door roused Calvin from the heavy sleep that had washed over him. He had slept for a long time too exhausted from the previous days to even worry about it. The knock came again and Calvin dragged himself to the door to see who had disturbed him. He half expected to see Airia and Mira so he grumbled slightly as he threw open the door, then turned red and begged apology.

Standing in his doorway was a man in what appeared to be a royal uniform. He appeared to be of about his own age and was striking in a royal blue uniform trimmed with gold, the gold setting off the highlights in his strawberry blonde curly hair. The uniform complemented his royal blue eyes that shone with an intense brilliance. He stood rigidly tall and had a serious look upon his face. "No need to apologize, sir, it is I that should apologize for disturbing you. I am a member of Eartheria's court and have been asked to summon you to her. Will you attend, sir?" He maintained his rigid stance waiting for Calvin's reply.

"Now? May I take a few minutes to get ready?" Calvin seemed taken aback at the request.

"Of course, take as long as you need I shall wait here for you." The courtier did not hesitate with his reply.

"Please come in and make yourself at home," Calvin offered, feeling awkward at someone standing outside his door.

"Thank you, sir," the gentleman stated, expressing his gratitude at not having to wait there as well.

Calvin motioned him in and a table of food appeared between the chairs filled with a hearty breakfast. "What is your name?" Calvin asked as he offered him a chair.

"Hans," he said.

"Well, Hans, enjoy." Calvin ate quickly then retired to bathe and dress in more suitable clothes. He chose a tunic of bright red satin with cream colored breeches; about his neck he fastened a velvet cape also in cream with golden threads around the edges. Calvin donned a pair of fawn colored boots in soft supple leather, which felt like air upon his feet. He looked regal if he said so himself, as he picked up his staff and sauntered through the doorway.

When he entered the outer room the courtier rose quickly and bowed as if Calvin was royalty to him. "Please, you don't have to do that," Calvin commented quickly. "Let us go, we have kept Eartheria waiting too long as it is." Hans opened the door and gestured to Calvin to follow him. Hallways curved and twisted about but Hans seemed to know his way. Calvin followed obediently, becoming a bit anxious until they stood in front of the familiar doors. Hans did not stop to announce him, which seemed a bit strange to Calvin, but when the doors opened and he stepped through he realized why. Eartheria was alone, pacing back and forth, almost in a panicked frenzy. "What is wrong?" Calvin rushed to her side.

"Airia and Mira have disappeared, both of them, sometime during the night." She looked at Calvin and he could see she had been crying. "We found these in the hall." Eartheria handed Calvin a feather and pieces of the girls' gowns. Calvin stood with his mouth open, gaping at the things Eartheria had passed his way.

"But—how," he finally sputtered.

"We do not know. We only know that they are gone and," she waved at the items in Calvin's hand "these things were in the hall it does not look good. Logan has shared your story with me, can you help us?"

"Of course, I just wish I knew where to begin." Calvin did not hesitate, they were his friends and he would find them, somehow.

"I will go with you." Hans stepped forward, offering his hand. "They were my friends as well," he choked.

"Then let us begin, take me to the spot these items were found." Calvin whirled around, he did not say anything more to Eartheria, he simply focused on the task at hand hurrying with Hans to the place where the girls had last been.

The hallways were wide but curved about in snakelike fashion, leaving many corners at which the girls could have been ambushed. After a time Hans pointed at the location. "There, in the center of the hall," he said. Calvin walked to the center and with Hans they began to explore the corridor, the walls, the floor, the ceiling. "There," Hans said, pointing at a small notch at the base of a gargoyle, "what is that?"

Calvin peered at the spot closely. "It looks like a catch of some kind, have you got a knife on you?" Hans handed Calvin a small blade and Calvin worked the point into the niche below the gargoyle, suddenly—a wall slid back and a dark passage led away from where they were. Calvin and Hans looked at each other then passed into the passage towards what lay ahead. Hans grabbed the candle from the gargoyles hands as he went. The passage was very narrow with cobwebs drooping from the walls where a previous occupant had swept them away. The dusty floor had scuffmarks upon it, so disorganized and chaotic that they could not tell how many people had passed this way.

"We have heard great things about you from Logan." Hans related to Calvin, breaking the awkward silence. "He says that if anyone can find the girls it is you."

"Thank you," Calvin said, "but it was with his help that we succeeded last time. Together perhaps we shall have success as well." Calvin clapped a hand on Hans' shoulder. They grinned at each other and continued on.

At a fork in the passage Calvin and Hans looked closely at the floor, it was difficult to tell which way they had gone, scuffmarks seemed to go in every direction. At last they settled on one branch of the passage and worked their way down it, the flickering of the candle casting eerie dancing images on the rough walls. Suddenly Hans stopped and Calvin ran into the back of him. "What is it?" he cried at the abrupt halt. Hans turned to the side to let Calvin's vision focus in front of him and there in the passage was a giant black hairy spider with yellow stripes down its legs. Huge pincers clipped together menacingly, warning them back along the path they had just followed. "Do you still think this is the direction that they came? We cannot get around this thing and we'll have to fight it. I just want to be sure that is necessary." Calvin cautioned Hans about the seriousness of the situation.

"I am certain, the markings were really disorganized and seemed to go everywhere but they seemed to lead in the end in this direction." Hans' determination did not waver.

"Well then, perhaps a brilliant flame will send this creature on his way." Calvin pushed past Hans and focused on the staff in his hand and thought of a brilliant flame of fire. His concentration wavered slightly and at first he thought he had failed but suddenly a bright light erupted from the tip. As the light increased an actual flame licked from the tip towards the spider in front of him. The spider's pincers clipped rapidly as it backed up through the passage slowly. Calvin inched forward towards the spider, maintaining his concentration on the flame. He envisioned the flame spewing from the tip of the staff like a flame-thrower, picturing it again, and again in his mind. Suddenly the flame blew out of the tip of the staff and the spider trapped within the tiny passage curled up from the flaring heat. Calvin tentatively moved towards the spider, unsure if it was truly dead and stepped gingerly around the mass of legs curled up about the spider's body, Hans followed suit and the trek down the corridor resumed.

Hans and Calvin emerged into a small room littered with debris. Along the wall on the right was a large wrought iron gate with a rusted lock fed through it. There did not appear to be anything but a small alcove beyond the gate and no being, living or dead was within it. Across the room was a solid looking wall with a gargoyle sconce upon the wall and an old candle draped with cob webs within its grasp. To the left stood a small wooden door, the latch and hinges worn and rusted but it appeared as though scuff marks were before it on the floor. Calvin hurried to the door and tried the latch, despite its appearance it moved freely and Calvin motioned Hans through. The room on this side was similar to the first however the alcove held the skeletal remains of its previous occupant. Hans and Calvin shuddered but like the first room there was only one other exit. They moved to the door and cautiously swung it open, this time leading into a short narrow passage. Both Hans and Calvin had to stoop slightly to pass through the tiny space into the room beyond.

Built within rock this room was neither circular nor square the walls bowed in places and straightened out in others, it could have passed for a natural cave and perhaps at one point it was. There were several columns roughly hewn supporting the ceiling above and a small wrought iron gate stood at the far left hand side of the room.

Hans walked over to the gate. "Calvin," he cried and Calvin ran to his side. There on the floor were two crumpled heaps, both unconscious lying on the earthen floor.

"Airia, Mira can you hear me?" Calvin was distraught at the sight. Neither mound moved.

"Help me with this lock." Calvin urged Hans and the two of them struggled at the lock in the gate. The lock was solid and old, made of a heavy metal, and bore the marks of many years of use. There was no key and nothing they could do would persuade the lock to open. "There has to be another way," Calvin cried. Hans began to search the outer room, every nook and cranny, looking for a key or something to pick the lock with. His search was futile.

"We'll have to continue on for the captors and regain the key," Hans said with conviction.

"I don't want to leave them alone," Calvin replied, "they have been through too much to wake up here."

"You can't go on alone, I won't let you!" Hans barked. "Together we will beat them alone, well, one never knows. Can you bring someone here? With your staff?" Calvin looked at him with an expression between disbelief and annoyance.

"No, the last time I tried that was when I tried to find Airia before and I wound up with her—not the other way around. We'll go together then; at least they have each other until we return." There was another small doorway in the room and both men ran to it, hurrying to find a way to retrieve their friends.

There was no door just the passageway, which led into another corridor that snaked around in a twisting path. They followed it for a while when suddenly a large bird appeared before them, sitting on a perch, shrouded with a bluish fog. An eagle, Calvin thought like the one outlined in the quest. Calvin recalled the message that he had first read.

A goblin dangerous magic makes
Stay away from the crafted cage
Shield the eyes from the eagles stare
The cage will break with a single blare

"Don't look at its eyes!" Calvin shouted violently at Hans.

Hans did a double take and looked at Calvin, "Wh-What?"

"Don't look at its eyes," Calvin repeated then filled Hans in on what exactly the quest had said.

Hans looked at the bird without looking at its eyes. The bird appeared harmless, but he did not want to risk whatever power it might possess.

"What do we do?" Hans asked, confused by the task that lay before them.

"I'm not sure," Calvin muttered. "Shield the eyes from the eagles stare, the cage will break with a single blare." Calvin's eyes roamed the room in front of them. There was the bird sitting on the perch in the middle of some blue fog, below his feet hung a golden horn. "We need that horn."

Hans joined Calvin in pursuit of the horn. They needed to be able to see the horn but not the bird and neither one of them knew how to accomplish this, the other factor to consider was the blue fog and neither wanted to know what its affect might take. "Calvin, can you create a wind with your staff, enough to move the blue fog?"

"I think so, but what about the bird, I can't focus on more than one thing, at least not more than one thing when I'm trying to do something." Calvin frequently thought of more than one thing when he wanted to go to the Glen or his suite but that was more of defining the place he wanted to be, adding the descriptive details. But to try and create a wind out of nothing and block the bird at the same time; that he was certain he would not be able to achieve.

Hans continued to look about the room. In a far corner he spotted a small mirror hung in a niche in the wall. The mirror was covered in filth and cob webs draped it in a curtain of silky threads. Hans lifted the mirror from the wall. It was heavier than it looked, but he held it firmly as he walked back by Calvin. "Here, this mirror I think will let us see the horn and the eagle without actually looking at it. It worked with Medusa anyway, why not give it a try?"

"Okay, but how are you going to use it? I need to know so I can be ready with whatever it might take."

"While you divert the fog I'll look in the mirror and walk backwards to the bird. Once I am there I can bend over to see the horn but be out of view of the eagles eyes, if I don't trip myself up first that is." Hans gave a short laugh. He was famous for tripping and falling over practically nothing, but this time he had to be on the money.

"Right, as soon as the fog is clear I'll signal you. Get ready!" Calvin exclaimed.

Hans stood at the ready with the mirror in front of his face and his body turned with his back to the bird. Calvin began his concentration on a wind strong enough to move the blue fog.

The wind started slowly as a gentle breeze then built to storm force winds and finally gale force winds. The fog did not move until the gale force winds began to blow and then the fog slowly moved back away from the bird. As soon as the bird was clear Calvin shouted, "Now!" and Hans started his backward trek to the bird. Hans had to keep stopping to get his bearings; somehow he needed to remind himself that what he was looking at in the mirror was reverse of what it actually was. Calvin had to keep the wind up to keep the fog back and Hans was bent over trying not to hurtle towards the bird with the wind. After what seemed like an eternity Hans had reached the bird. He bent further forward then swung around under the bird, his head just barely clearing the perch above him. The horn swung on a leather tether from the perch above. Hans reached up carefully aided with the mirror and undid the strap from the perch. When the horn was safely in his hands he bolted away from the bird toward where Calvin stood. Calvin stopped the wind almost immediately after Hans was clear of the bird and the fog gently rolled back into position about the feathery fiend.

With the horn in hand the two travelers hurried back along the path they had come to the room where the alcove held the two girls. The girls were up, holding onto each other and softly crying. "Calvin!" they shouted in unison. "Hans! How did you find us? How long have you been here?" Hundreds of questions washed over them as they tried to comprehend just what had happened to them.

"We'll go over that in a minute, stand as far away from the gate as possible, we're going to get you out of there but we're not sure this will work." Calvin tried to sound positive but they really did not know if what they were about to try would work.

"Plug your ears as tightly as you can," Hans called out to them.

Quickly the girls covered their ears and Hans did the same as

Calvin put the horn to his lips. He played trumpet, but this horn was different from what he had, the principle was the same, so with a deep breath he blew into the horn sending a reverberating noise about the small room. They watched in amazement as the gate in front of the alcove began to crack then shattered into thousands of little pieces. As soon as the gate broke, Calvin stopped playing the horn, and he and Hans ran over the rubble to the two frightened girls.

The girls flung themselves at the two boys, happy to be released from the prison where they had been held, and hugged the boys until each thought his breath would never return. Gasping they gently pried themselves loose from the tight hold and said in unison, "You're okay now. You're safe." The girls started babbling, asking questions by the dozens and the boys laughed at the confusion all the questions made.

"Let's get out of here, and then we can talk," muttered Calvin. "I'd like to get as far away from here as we can, somewhere safe." Hans nodded in complete agreement and each boy took the arm of a girl and started back from where they came. The girls shuddered violently when they had to step over the carcass of the dead spider, revolted at the sight of the mangled beast. The way was longer than Hans and Calvin remembered, but Calvin did not want to risk trying to get away with magic with so many people involved. He was weary from the strain the wind had made on him and the horn had winded him as well.

When they reached the corridor of the castle, Hans led them back to Calvin's suite. There they told the girls the pieces of the tale, embellishing only what seemed quite boring in the way that boys do, and fitted the pieces of the puzzle together for the two girls. Calvin thought about food for the first time since his breakfast feast and realized it must be well into dinner, they had missed their mid-day meal. He pulled the chairs in front of the sofa and quickly envisioned a table laden with food. The table appeared as always and the four feasted on the savory dishes, each of them famished from the long day.

What seemed, to Calvin, to be hours later, the others finally retired to their own quarters, leaving him free to sleep. He retreated to the bath and sank into the luxurious tub, letting the water cascade over his aching muscles. He fell asleep where he was, relaxed from the pulsing sensation of the warm water. He slept well for a time, but all too soon a haunting dream broke into his thoughts and he woke with a start, sinking abruptly into the water surrounding him. He rose distractedly and retired to his bed. Climbing into the bed he let the soft pillows billow about him and pulled the comforter nearly over his head, but as he drifted off to sleep the cushiony comfort that surrounded him faded away and he began to dream.

The leathery gray skin of a beast twisted in fury blazing a fiery stream of flames upon the lush green carpet of a wooded glade, the trees erupting into an inferno that left nothing but charred and blackened remains. A beautiful maiden sat upon a throne of golden cherubs, laughing hideously with each breath the beast made. The beast roared, pulling its head back in an arch of contempt and hurled another lethal blast at the helpless landscape…

Calvin jolted awake, the horror of his vision blotting out where he truly was. Moments passed before he woke fully enough to realize he had been dreaming. It was a nightmare. He could not help wondering what part he would play in the dream for his previous dreams had turned into reality. He lay in bed catching his scattered breath and tried to think of something else. His thoughts turned to home, to his family, to his mother. He wished that he had not been so anxious to see what was in the chest. If he had left it alone he would not be here, but if he had left it alone he would not have been here to save Airia, or Mira and he would not have met Logan or Hans. He thought of Eartheria who, like his mother, worried about the inhabitants of her land.

Slowly he awoke into the day, dressed in a muted tunic of soft gray with pants in a deep gray, the clothes he chose mirroring his mood. The cape matched the breeches in color and hid the fabric of the clothes beneath. He slunk out into the outer room, dragging his feet as he went, weary physically and mentally. He plopped into the chair near the fire draping a leg over the arm of the chair. His mother would have had a fit to see him lounging over the edge of the chair like that. He moved his leg with that thought and decided to move to the sofa where he could stretch out in more comfort. He sat there for a while watching the flames of the fire and not really thinking of anything. Finally he rose and thought about breakfast. The fare this morning was meager like his enthusiasm for the day, muffins with jams and jellies, tea and fresh fruit; Calvin didn't even seem to notice he was so absorbed in his thoughts.

A sharp knock on the door interrupted his thoughts and he moved to the door to open it. Hans stood at the door, looking regal in his uniform denoting his station within the castle walls. "Hi, Calvin, gees—you look down this morning—what's the matter?"

Calvin looked at Hans and simply said, "Miss my mother."

Hans gave a nod of understanding then moved toward the center of the room. "Eartheria sent me to fetch you. Are you able to meet with her today? It seems there is something else troubling her; you two make a good pair, always worrying about something."

"Yeah—sure," Calvin remarked. "Let me grab my things and we'll be on our way." Calvin reached for his staff and grabbed the small pouch of herbs Logan had given him. He would be thankful later that he did.

Chapter 10

Calvin plodded down the hall after Hans, still dragging his feet like earlier. He did not seem to have any ambition this morning and he never seemed to get enough rest. He supposed he sounded ungrateful for their hospitality but he wished he could just sit down and do nothing for a whole day, or at least play some video games. He supposed his mother had been right about his being hooked on them but it was the way things were at home, all his friends played them and he looked at them like his mother looked at a good book, a means of escape.

Well he certainly didn't need "*escape*" here. There was enough excitement and danger to keep any boredom from setting in. Here the thought of nothing to do was like a dream come true.

Hans pushed the door of Eartheria's room open. Inside he found her pacing back and forth deep in thought. Calvin slunk into the room also deep in thought and Hans shook his head at the two of them. He glanced in one more time then backed out of the room and shut the door.

"Calvin, I'm glad you could come," Eartheria said, grasping his hand. "I have a very uneasy feeling; I'm not sure what it is. I thought perhaps if I spoke with you there might be something you know that would explain it."

"Uh, hmm—well I don't really know anything, but you are right to feel uneasy. I had a dream last night, a nightmare really, and it began like this...

The leathery gray skin of a beast twisted in fury blazing a fiery stream of flames upon the lush green carpet of a wooded glade, the trees erupting into an inferno that left nothing but charred and blackened remains. A beautiful maiden sat upon a throne of golden cherubs laughing hideously with each breath the beast made. The beast roared pulling its head back in an arch of contempt and hurled another lethal blast at the helpless landscape…

Eartheria shuddered with uncontrolled fear, her eyes wide with fright and turmoil. "What is it all about? Where could it be?" Eartheria shuddered again visibly distraught at the descriptive dream. She paced once again her brow knitted in furrows of deep concentration.

Calvin knew the depth of her fear for his feelings were not far behind. "Can Hans go with me?" he asked, hopeful of his company once again. "And Logan, we may need him."

Logan's knowledge of herbs was invaluable to him and if anyone should be injured Calvin wanted to make certain he was with them.

"Yes, of course, I shall summons him. What will you need? Where are you going?" Eartheria looked at Calvin with concern.

"To the forest, I'm going to try to transport us there. If I succeed we will be in the location we need to be, if I fail, who knows..." Calvin did not sound very hopeful and he certainly did not seem like he had a plan, but to Eartheria he sounded like a man with courage, courage to face his fear and courage to face the unknown.

"I'll send for them then, I'll ask them to come to your quarters you can leave from there. God's blessings on your voyage, Calvin!" Eartheria turned from him not willing to let him see the tears in her eyes. Calvin turned and strode from the room, finding his way back to his quarters with only minimal difficulty. He set about preparing sacks of supplies, two of them heavier than the third and he rounded up three short swords and lightweight shields. He knew this time what he faced but he did not know the ultimate danger of the place. He only hoped that the supplies they took would be enough.

Knocking sharply on the door Hans waited for Calvin to answer. Only a moment passed and the door swung open and Calvin beckoned him into the room. Hans stepped into the inner room carrying some things he had brought for their journey for Eartheria had filled him in on the quest ahead. He understood the importance of being prepared and the dangers they would face. When Eartheria had summoned him he had not expected to be sent on such an important mission, he was both excited and apprehensive, what lay before them could mean death, but it could also mean a great adventure.

"Hi, Hans, ready for another adventure?" Calvin clapped Hans playfully on the shoulder, showing more enthusiasm then he felt.

"You bet," Hans returned, jabbing him back. "Logan should be coming as well, but the way is a bit more difficult for him to get here."

Calvin looked at his watch out of habit and shrugged, it had stopped working the moment he had set foot in this world and it had not started working again so it was pointless really to look at it. The two set about adding the supplies that Hans had brought to the sacks Calvin had packed. Calvin told Hans which sack was for whom so that Hans would not overload Logan's sack, the way would be difficult enough for him.

A tapping noise on the door alerted the two that their friend had arrived and sure enough Logan stood at the entrance beaming with excitement. He couldn't knock on the door exactly as his arms were full of herbs and assundries of various kinds. Hans and Calvin laughed out loud; he looked funny poking his head up about the herbs he carried, and shaking their heads they rearranged the sacks once again, trying to accommodate everything they felt they just had to have. Once they were settled they had a quick discussion to finalize their plans for their journey then together they put on their warm cloaks, fastened the scabbards in place, belted the pouches of herbs and slung their sacks over their backs. With that accomplished Calvin picked up the staff and all three placed their hands about its curving surface while Calvin concentrated on his dream.

The leathery gray skin of a beast twisted in fury blazing a fiery stream of flames upon the lush green carpet of a wooded glade, the trees erupting into an inferno that left nothing but charred and blackened remains. A beautiful maiden sat upon a throne of golden cherubs laughing hideously with each breath the beast made. The beast roared pulling its head back in an arch of contempt and hurled another lethal blast at the helpless landscape...

The suite of rooms grew vague and foggy and soon the three travelers found themselves surrounded by trees. The wooded glade was not nearly as dense as the woods about the Glen, the trees interspersed with stretches of green and light filtering through in arcs and swaths in a bright colorful array. Little patches of flowers poked up here and there and the glade smelled fresh and fragrant. There really wasn't much of a path to speak of, just trails scampering about in a random fashion like a deer flitting through the woods. It was peaceful and Calvin found it hard to believe that it was the same glade contained in his horrible dream.

They wandered about for a while, getting a feel of the lay of the land. The glade was large many miles in all directions and roamed freely among little hills and valleys. The vast expanse was covered in trees but here and there a small clearing poked its head out of the woods as if to breath. If faced with a dragon's breath however, there really was not a stronghold to offer much cover. A noise from across the glade surprised them and they noted a small cabin, perhaps a room or too, on the far side. It was covered with vines and looked as if no one had visited the dwelling in many years. They walked across the glade and stepped onto the rotting porch, boards cracked and missing making a dismal welcome mat. Together they shouldered the door open and field mice scampered from the room. Dust and dirt lay upon the floor and here and there a stray weed sprouted from the cracks and grew in disarray. There was a fireplace full of ash and old embers and a small wooden table with a stool but besides that the place was empty. "Well, it's little better than a roof over our heads, but it will have to do," Logan said, giving his appraisal of the dismal quarters. "I'll see if I can't get a fire going, it'll be cold soon."

While Logan worked on the hearth the other two gathered some weeds from the field, bound them about the top and used them to sweep the grime from the floor. They sneezed and coughed as the dust rolled into the air with the first strokes, but persevered until the floor somewhat resembled clean. There was no water about that they had found so they would need to conserve what they had for drinking, sparing none to be clean.

They opened their packs and splayed the contents about, clumping items of similar use together. The food they set upon the table still with a sack to protect it from the filth still present in the room. A small fire finally blazed in the hearth and Logan perused the room with little more than disgust. "I'll see what I can do in here, you two see if you can find a source of water and somewhere a bit sturdier than this for home base. If it's a dragon we face this place will be tinder. Don't be long though it will be night soon."

Calvin and Hans wandered around the back of the cabin. Here the woods were a bit denser and a cool breeze caught through the trees, rippling them and giving the boys a chill. They sauntered into the woods, carefully marking their way, finding shards of pottery here and there, once they found a complete bowl and tucked it into a sack to take back to the shack. A voice called to them from the distance, a musical voice, beckoning them on. Calvin put his hand out and stopped Hans in his tracks. "NO!" he cried, "it is a trap."

Hans looked at the serious expression on Calvin's face and scowled "What makes you so sure?"

"It's a gut feeling but I think it is the last of the quest" Calvin shook his head to clear his thoughts "listen..."

A dragon's breath will sear your heart
Beware the temptress from the start
Set ablaze the midnight skies
The dragon breath to no more rise

"It is her, I'm certain of it and I don't have any intention of being led into her trap." Calvin looked at Hans with pleading eyes, but Hans had already made up his mind, Calvin had good instincts and he wasn't about to ignore them.

Walking quickly back to the cabin Calvin and Hans tried to think of a way to protect themselves from the dragon when it came. They didn't have anything in their sacks, except for their shields that even remotely could withstand heat. Engrossed in their conversation neither of them saw the tiny squirrelly creature that darted in and out of the branches of the trees, neither that is until a loud slap sent them spinning on their heels towards the noise.

"Look out, Calvin! Those are squirrelly scags, vicious little creatures that will gnaw anything in their way." Hans pulled the sword from its scabbard. "A sword won't be much good against them we should hurry away from here." Hans' statement jolted Calvin to the fact that other dangers lay about besides the dragon and they would need to continue to be on the alert and ready for anything.

Calvin drew his sword and with his back against Hans' they edged sideways toward the cabin, the squirrelly scags darting about in a furious frenzy. The little beasts darted in and out and the two boys had to swing quickly and accurately to stave off the attack. The fighting was fierce and quick and before they knew it the battle was over, for the moment at least. They raced to the cabin, out of breath; there they collapsed on the porch away from the scene of the foray. Their breath slowed and they rose to enter the cabin. Logan noticed the state of Calvin and Hans and motioned them to sit. He brought them a warm mug of tea then waited patiently for them to relate their tale. He was not surprised by the creatures inhabiting the wood and seemed almost relieved to hear it was nothing worse. They told him of the voice singing in the woods and the reasons why they had turned back.

"It was wise of you to retreat for surely the voice was that of the temptress. I've heard fables of her and the magical web she weaves," Logan mused. "We must remain alert and sharpen our senses to what lies ahead. We must leave this place in the morning, I have a deep sensation of formidable danger; it would not be wise for us to linger here."

"We did not see any place of value behind the cabin in the direction of the east, tomorrow we shall head north to see if we fare any better." Calvin tried to sound somewhat hopeful. The weary travelers crashed upon their capes on the still dusty floor and slept for it would be time soon enough when sleep would not be possible.

Rising early they gathered their belongings and set out toward the north, the landscape very similar to that of the day before. They walked for what seemed like miles resting briefly when they were tired. Finally they came to what appeared to be a solid rock wall climbing into a steep mountain. They did not proceed forward but rather followed the wall towards the west, trying to avoid the enchantress in the east. With the rocks on their right and the trees on their left they moved steadily along. At one point a spring bubbled up from the ground and they stooped to replenish their water. Stopping for a much needed rest, they set their sacks upon the ground and Logan took out biscuits and jam for them to eat and there was jerky as well, the boys munched hungrily on several pieces.

"The rocks are thinning, the mountain dwindling to a pile of rubble from here. Perhaps in the outcropping we will be able to secure some sort of fortress," Hans acknowledged.

Calvin glanced about and agreed, pointing out a potential cluster near them. "That looks promising."

Hans and Logan looked in the direction Calvin was pointing. "Good possibility," they said.

When they were done eating the three meandered over to the pile of rocks and began assessing the situation. There was a slight overhang that afforded some protection and with some manipulation of the stones surrounding it they could create a so called home of stone. With great effort the two young boys started moving boulders about, clearing some flat stones beneath and piling the others in a crude wall but left an opening for a door while Logan used smaller stones to build a pit for fire to be used for cooking. Calvin and Hans wandered a little into the forest and rummaged enough evergreen boughs to make a rustic roof, but if it kept rain out that was all that mattered. Upon the completion of their new quarters the three stepped back to survey the work they had done.

"Not bad—" Logan exclaimed admiringly. "It is a far sight better than the cabin and at least it will not go up like a match, should the dragon strike it, warm yes—but disregarding the roof generally intact. The spring near by is a plus as well, we will be able to replenish our water and it might come in handy against a stray fire as well."

Calvin laughed. "Only if the stray fire is the size of a campfire perhaps." All three chuckled and they set about, gathering boughs to sleep on. When they were finished three crudely crafted cots were set about the tiny area. They did not try to set them under the overhang as they might need that area when the dragon arrived and did not want anything in the way to trip them up.

"We should form a plan for when the dragon does rouse its head," Hans suggested, and so they sat around their rock table, a piece of parchment between them and created a plan of attack or defense, whichever way you looked at it. The plan was not much but at least it gave them some sense of preparedness. They bedded down for some rest waiting for the inevitable. Soft music wafted into the house of stone, a feminine voice, soft and provocative, singing an eerie tune. Calvin, Hans and Logan awoke and rubbed the sleep from their eyes.

"Don't listen, here wad this in your ears." Calvin handed Logan and Hans some soft batting he had torn from a pillow. Carefully they wedged the cottony material in their ears blocking out the sound of the singing. Logan moved to the fire in the pit they had created and placed a pot of water on to boil, Hans to the door with his sword drawn, and Calvin stepped on a rock near the table and poked his head through a gap in the makeshift roof.

In the forest stood a beautiful woman picking flowers, her mouth moved as if she was singing, but the batting in his ears kept Calvin from hearing the tune. He looked beyond her and saw a large shadow soar across the glade then fade then return once again, the dragon, he was sure of it. He used hand motions to signal Hans and Logan of the impending danger, carefully they began the preparations for their plan. Moving quietly with the staff firmly held within his hand Calvin moved toward the center of their encampment, the hole in the roof above the fire would be his window to the sky. Hans maintained his stance at the door his sword held out in front of him ready to strike anything which might make his way to the door. Logan extinguished the fire quickly and quietly, with hardly any smoke escaping from it, then moved under the overhang and spread out his herbs.

The enchantress must have sensed something unfamiliar for suddenly her lips stilled and a crooked smile whisked across her face. She moved her mouth again and signaled with her hands, the dragon familiar with the signal coughed a stream of white, hot fire below where black billowy smoke erupted from the woods and the temptress threw her head back as if in a laugh. The temptress swayed and motioned all the while with her lips moving in a chant the others could not hear because of the cotton wadded in their ears. Her long hair swelled out about her head, her face contorted in an evil grimace, jet black eyes darker than coal itself shone with a twisted glitter as if they mirrored the horror about to unfold.

Calvin focused all his energy on the staff, he thought of the sun, large and round, blistering hot on a bright summer day in the middle of the tropics. Not a cloud was in the sky and the blazing sun seemed to sear the surface of everything below it. As he thought images of the beach wandered into his mind with the sun blazing brightly above it. He continued to focus on the sun bringing it nearer, larger, and hotter than molten lava. Hans wiped his brow the warmth within the stone walls building to unbearable heights, he glanced at Logan under the overhang but he seemed to be fairing slightly better. Perhaps the enclosure was cooled from the depths of the mountain itself.

Another blast erupted in the woods, charring the previously serene setting. The blaze rebounded off the rocks and the thatch of the roof began to burn, as the roof reached an inferno, pieces fell within the stone walls, one landed on Hans' arm. He jerked back instinctively then retreated back to the outcropped rock and sheltered with Logan under the overhang. Logan began to attend his wounds with the skill of a physician. They were trapped now; all their hope hinged on Calvin. As he worked his magic the others waited—thinking of the written quest Calvin had found.

A dragon's breath will sear your heart
Beware the temptress from the start
Set ablaze the midnight skies
The dragon breath to no more rise

A huge crash shuddered through the forest rippling waves through the ground sending shocks through the walls that surrounded them. Instinctively their hands went out as if to balance them but as quickly as it had started it stopped and all became still. Hans moved back to the doorway and looked outside. There in the woods among the charred remains of the trees was the body of the dragon, a hideous mass of twisted gray, small wisps of smoke curling up from the surface. The temptress through back her head and howled an unearthly kind of howl, the noise loud enough to filter through the batting stuffed in their ears. They clamped their hands to the sides of their head to shut out the tormented scream. While they watched the temptress began to vaporize, fading at first then becoming a fine mist, until finally the particles dispersed into the air. It was over.

Chapter 11

Caught between relief and the loss of excitement the three travelers looked out between the stone walls and sighed, a deep cleansing sigh. The gravest of dangers was over and they could now go home. Calvin, more than the others, thought of home with a new found sense of appreciation, for with the quest over he could truly go home, not to the suite he had occupied in this land of no time, but to his home with his mother and father and all of his friends.

For now however, they would need to return to the castle in the mountain, to Hans' world, to Logan's world. He looked at the other two. "Let's go home!" he said with conviction in his heart. Logan and Hans agreed heartily ready to leave the devastation behind, where the new trees would rise up from the ashes, clumps of flowers springing up between, creating a new wooded glade fresh and untarnished.

They quickly packed their sacks then, each in turn, took hold of the staff. Calvin thought of the suite he occupied, of all of the details in the outer room and soon they stood there with the hearth blazing brightly and the candles on the mantle. They celebrated their victory with food, with laughter and with the girls they had left behind. Even Eartheria joined in the joyous celebration, contentment finally visible on her face.

With mixed emotions Calvin said his good-byes for he had come to a close relationship with his new found friends, his leaving bittersweet in his mind. Eartheria told him that he must return through the corridor to the place where he had entered and with the staff in his hand he would now be able to think of home and return from where he began. She told him too that the clothes he had come with would be in the wardrobe of his bedroom. Calvin went to the other room and just as she had said his former clothes hung within the wardrobe. He changed quickly suddenly very aware of his long sleeve tee and jeans, the cold without the cloak seeping into his bones. When he put on his sneakers however, Calvin suddenly longed for the soft kidskin boots he had grown accustomed to. Wadding his down jacket under his arm he ventured into the outer room and everyone looked a bit shocked for they had not seen him in the clothes he normally wore.

"We'll go with you as far as the beginning of the corridor," Hans said.

"Wear your cloak at least until then, it will keep the chill off for a while," Logan quipped handing him the warm cloak. Airia and Mira tried to hold the smiles on their faces but Calvin could see the sadness behind them.

They walked slowly to the end of the corridor leading down the mountain, lingering longer than they should have near the passageway. In the end Calvin continued on alone, down the corridor, down the stairs back to the place from which he had come. He kept the cloak on, not wanting to part from the warmth it provided and wanting to hold on to a piece of this timeless place.

When he reached the spot, or at least as near to it as he could recall, Calvin thought of the barn, of the odd assortment of old junk, of the cobwebs and dust, and of his friend Matt. The familiar sensation of fading returned and this time he found himself standing in his own time, the staff still firmly gripped within his hand. Matt peered at the chest as if Calvin had never left. "It's useless," he said, "The chest is hopelessly locked."

Calvin nodded his head and laughed… "Let's go back to the house, it's freezing in here."

Matt looked at Calvin then suddenly said, "Hey—where'd you get the cool cape?" Calvin had forgotten that he was wearing it.

"Behind the chest," he said, trying to sound convincing. "While you were in the other room, pretty neat, huh?"

"Yeah, you going to keep it?" Matt asked.

"Yep," was all Calvin said.

They clambered over the junk strewn about in the barn then raced across the field back to the house, the smell of fresh baked apple pie wafting on the air. They dumped their jackets in the coatroom at the back of the house then entered the kitchen, their cheeks pink from the chill of the outside air, where his mom greeted them.

"How about some hot chocolate?" she asked them. The boys eagerly nodded and she handed them both a steaming mug. "Some friends stopped by while you were in the barn, they're waiting in the living room."

Calvin looked at Matt and shrugged in confusion. As they walked into the living room Calvin stopped, his heart skipping a beat or two. There in the middle of his living room were Hans, Mira and Airia and Calvin was suddenly very glad; as happiness overwhelmed him his thoughts turned to the future and the adventures they would have.

Printed in the United States
47401LVS00006B/343-351